I0760532

PROVIDENTIAL PRESS

presents

WHERE the WATER RISES

a TALE of LOVE & SACRIFICE

A.T. LISCHAK

For permissions requests, contact the author at this email: author@atlischak.com

Hardcover ISBN: 978-1-963275-08-7
Softcover ISBN: 978-1-963275-06-3

Third Edition

TABLE OF CONTENTS

LISTEN ALONG
with the
AUDIOBOOK

free on podcasts including
APPLE & SPOTIFY

for my mother and father,
whom I love very much

PART I
THE TOWN

The boy held his mother's hand close to his chest. It was cold. *She* was dying.

But not yet. There was still life in her eyes. And those, Jordan knew, were still warm.

He loved looking at them. They were the bluest he had ever seen. Like living waters. But when he came to think of it, those were just about the *only* eyes he had ever seen.

You see, he lived alone with his mother. Together, they lived far in the woods, close to the mountains. His whole life, he knew to play only so far from home. There was a small open meadow near the back, and he was pretty happy there. He was ten now. So those memories of other people had almost faded away completely by this point.

She made life worth living for Jordan. When she wasn't washing and cleaning and cooking and teaching and all the other things mothers do, she'd go outside and find Jordan running in the tall grass. She'd go out there and play with him. And she'd smile and laugh, which made Jordan even happier. He often thought her white teeth were almost as beautiful as her eyes. Really, it was hard to compare. He loved every part of her.

That was why it made him very sad to see her in bed. To find those eyes closed most of the time. To hardly ever get a glimpse of those teeth that were now well-hidden behind those bruised-looking lips.

He didn't know what to do. He hadn't been in this situation before. But he understood. His mother's condition didn't spring on them like a cold. He first noticed it about a year ago. He had reached for his mother's hand as they walked along a well-worn path to find her fingers like ice. He quickly let go, maybe because the coldness surprised him. Or perhaps it was because he didn't want to think about why his mother's usually warm hands weren't that way.

Jordan thought that, over time, they would return to normal. That when she petted his cheek or rubbed his neck, he'd suddenly find them to be as soothing as touching a steaming cup of cider. But they never did seem to come back. It was like her hands had somehow frozen over and died. He hadn't known that this frost would spread. Not at first.

She wore many blankets as she lay there. A fire was even burning in the fireplace. It *was* warm, Jordan thought to himself. But those hands of hers...always so cold.

He often sat by her side, especially nowadays. It had been a good long while since he played in the back meadow. But he'd rather be where his mother was, in that dim-lit room. Sitting and watching and waiting on her. He liked it when she opened her eyes, and they could talk together. She was still able to make him smile.

But *this* conversation was different. Her voice remained light and soft and gentle as ever. But the words that came out of her mouth felt dark and firm and harsh.

"Medicine," she said. And that was when he knew.

"You told me not to follow the road," said Jordan.

"Things change, Jo."

Jordan understood. But he was no less scared. It was true that all the medicine was now gone from the bathroom cabinet. His mother had finished everything.

She would always go to town alone if they were in need, but she'd been in bed for over three months now. Thankfully, his mother had been wise and bought more than they needed at the time. But now, as she well told him, things had changed.

It was hard to ignore that the pantry was almost empty. Jordan had begun to eat only twice a day. Then, it became once with a little snack near bedtime. Sometimes, he would skip an entire day to feed his mother a very big bowl of soup. Those days didn't seem so bad to him since he believed this would help his mother get better.

But she didn't get better. And now she was telling him to follow the road. Where did it lead?

He didn't know, exactly. But Jordan trusted his mother. *That*, he did know.

"Don't speak to anyone," she said. "And if they speak to you, just nod, or shake your head, or smile. And keep your distance." She handed him a folded-up sheet of paper and cupped her frozen hands over his. "And if they try to get near you, run."

Before he left, she pointed to the windowsill. A tall glass of water stood underneath the dull sunlight. He brought it over to her. She looked eager to drink it. Even as sick as she was, that cold glass of water went down faster than his warm soup had done.

"And don't drink the water, whatever you do."

Yes, he knew this. It was the first rule that was ever given to him. And how could he forget now? They had large basins around the yard to catch rainwater, and that was what Jordan drank from. Though he had always seen his mother drink from the tap, he never questioned why *he* never could.

Well, one time, he did. But all she told him was, "You'll die." And that was enough to keep him away. And quiet, too.

Jordan leaned in and kissed his mother. It was like kissing the snow. Then, he left with that piece of paper and no money and no one but himself. For the first time, he did not want to open the door that led outside.

He looked back and saw those blue eyes from the other room. And then, he saw those white teeth of hers, and he felt warm. And strangely happy. And so, he opened the door and stepped outside. Leaving his mother for the first time. *Really* leaving her. But he would be back. At least, he was set on it.

The air was wild and cold. The sunny blue sky lied to him, but that was not a big problem. Jordan had his jacket and his mother's scarf to keep him comfortable.

The path was made of dirt, and it bent this way and that. Yellow and orange and red leaves feathered down on him from time to time as he went. Other times, he caught animals watching him. Squirrels and birds and, at one point, a doe. None of these alarmed him.

But eventually, there came a part where the path ended. It hit another path. A darker, harder one. *The road.* Jordan had never been this far. But he remembered what his mother said and turned to the right.

A scare came when he heard a gurgling noise behind him. At first, it was faint. But it grew and grew. Jordan finally turned around to find a car tumbling down the road toward him.

He ducked behind the tree line and waited until it passed. Jordan had only seen a car once in his life. That was the time when his father got lost and never came back. Someone from town had come to tell his mother. Jordan had watched that car and that stranger from the attic window. Since then, he hadn't seen a car. Or another person. Just his mother. It'd been seven years.

The second strange thing that Jordan noticed was the smell of the air. It changed. It was like he pressed his nose in his mother's garden. There, she grew different types of herbs. One of them was wormwood. It was bitter and strong. And it made Jordan wrinkle his nose in dislike.

Eventually, he came up to a sign: *Brookfield.* He liked that he could read. His mother read to him every day before she got sick. And nowadays, he read to his mother. He never came across the word *Brookfield* before.

Jordan mouthed the word, saying it a few times to himself as he continued along the roadside. And then he saw it. Buildings. *A town.* A town apparently called Brookfield. He remembered this was the point in his journey where his mother told him to hide. To walk within the tree line. To edge around the back of buildings. To creep along alleyways. To not be seen.

Jordan did as he was told. The bitter smell grew stronger with every step. The sight of dingy brick walls and the sound of gravel under his feet made him think of the color grey.

He was almost there. Jordan tucked his head out from the shaded alley. In front of him was the town square. And in the middle, a large well. Perhaps that was the place where that awful stench came from. Just beyond it was another place. *The* place. The medicine shop. His destination.

How was he supposed to get from *here* to *there*? Jordan had to cross at some point. And now was probably his best chance. There was no one. Not a hint of life. With his heart beating hard, he stepped out into the open and crept toward the shop. He felt safe enough. But he still turned his head as he went, looking for anyone who might be watching.

Jordan had to pass the well to get to the medicine shop. He decided to stop. His head peered over the stony ridge. It was dark down there in the well. But his suspicion was right. The smell came from it. From deep down in there.

The odd thing was that the longer Jordan stood where he was, the sweeter the smell became. Eventually, he found himself quite relaxed. And also quite...*thirsty*. And so he kept leaning on the well and smelling the water below. But then he began to hear faint noises. Flickering of movement in the corner of his eyes. He looked up. There was someone in the distance, watching him. To his left, he found two more. Jordan caught a third one staring out her second-floor window. No one looked happy. At least, that's the way Jordan saw it. So he went on from that place.

The bell that hung over the door of the medicine shop rang. He quickly let himself inside. It smelled much different from the outside. Here, it smelled better. Not fresh, but definitely… *sanitized.*

He wasn't surprised to see the people pause to stare at him. Why was everyone doing this? Maybe it was because he was new. He had never seen any of them before, which meant they had never seen him, either.

Jordan came to the counter where a woman in white was waiting on the other side. She was bulky. Not like his mother, who seemed to thin over time. This woman's hair was pulled back in a bun. But he preferred the way his mother did hers. She always had it down, letting it wave and curl below her shoulders. Maybe Jordan was expecting all women to look like that. He now knew this was not the case.

Even though the woman did not have a smile on her face, she did seem safe to come near. But, of course, she was staring at him, too.

Jordan remembered what his mother said. To give the woman in white the slip of paper. He quickly searched his coat pockets and found it inside his right. Their hands touched as he passed it to her. Chills ran up Jordan's arm. She felt cold, too.

Her eyes left Jordan's to read the slip. After about half a minute, they returned. The woman's lips tightened. Her eyebrows moved closer together. Then, she breathed in and went to the back room, leaving Jordan to wait at the counter.

When he looked back to see if all the people were watching, he realized they seemed nearer to him now. But what was he supposed to do? His mother told him to run if they came too close, but the door was on the other side of the store. And he needed that medicine first.

Jordan found himself tapping his foot on the wooden floor. He was nervous. A minute passed into two, which rolled into three. He began forming an escape plan in his head while the clock went around a fourth. He didn't want to be there for a fifth.

But, to his relief, the woman did come back. A small, brown paper bag was in her fist. She handed it to him. Jordan shook it. Yep, medicine.

Just as he was about to walk away, the woman placed a thin, plastic cup on the counter.

"You look thirsty," she said. This comment

sounded odd, but maybe the woman was just concerned.

He looked around the room. Everyone seemed to be waiting for him to grab it.

"No, thanks," he said as kindly as he could.

"But you're breathing so heavy," said the woman. "Are you sure?"

Yes, he was. But what was he going to say? All he thought he could do at this point was smile. So he did. But he didn't wait to see what might happen next. He went off. The bag was placed safely inside his coat first. Then, he moved toward the door without delay, keeping his head down as he passed the staring strangers.

The bell rang again as he exited into the square. More people. *Great.* His eyes scanned from one end of the town to the other. He could try hugging the buildings until he made it safely to the other side. Maybe he could slip into an alley and find another roundabout way. But in the end, he went straight. Ahead of him was that narrow alleyway that he had come from. He knew that way led back home. And, if this helped him make the decision, it was the *quickest* way.

So he went for it. Jordan tried walking calmly across the pavement. It was hard to do. He badly wanted to sprout wings and fly.

He passed the well without stopping. And now, he was almost there. To the other side.

Then, he saw them. A group of boys, maybe a little older. Some, definitely a little fatter. Stronger. And they were moving in on him. He could see it in the corner of his eye.

And so he bolted. Jordan was right. They were after him. He could hear the gravel crunching rapidly behind him. *This* was a chase. He had never been in a chase, except if he counted hide and seek with his mother. But this felt very different.

Jordan chose not to take the road. He went straight into the forest. Maybe he thought the boys would be too scared to follow him there. After all, there were strange noises. Sometimes, it frightened *him*, too.

Jordan ran on for several minutes. It felt like miles to him. He didn't know where he was now. All he saw were trees from every angle. But then, he felt a shove. Jordan collapsed harshly onto twigs and branches that lay dead in the wood. A boy had tackled him. And he could feel that he wasn't going to be let go anytime soon.

Jordan struggled as they turned him over on his back. One of them held a bottle of water in his hand. Jordan begged them not to do it.

But the other boys just laughed. Were they laughing at his crying face? His eyes filled with fear? His lack of strength? Maybe it was all of that.

Jordan's arms were pinned down. He knew this meant the end. Like his mother said, to drink the water meant death. He understood now why he was never allowed to walk with her into town. Why he had to hide in the attic when people came to visit. Why the meadow and his tiny little house were all he ever knew. He wished he could go back there now. To go back in time. To forget everything that was happening at this moment.

But he knew he couldn't do that. If anything, his mother was on the edge of death herself. She needed the medicine more than anything. There was no other real choice, was there?

But if she were to die, and if he were to die, maybe they would see each other again, he thought. Perhaps they would be able to smile together. Jordan liked that idea. Not the part where both of them died. But the part where both of them would be close. Where they would be able to hold hands. And hers would be warm, at last. Yes, he did like that thought.

The boys taunted poor Jordan as he tried to move himself free. They made sure to open the bottle slowly. To drip it on his face. Over his eyes. Down his chest.

One of the boys ripped the paper bag from its hiding spot. With what Jordan thought was an ugly smile, that boy tore the cap off and flung all the pills far into the distance. Jordan watched as all strength left him. Those pills were soon lost under the bed of leaves and twigs and branches. Gone. His mother's only hope.

This made him angry. It helped him find his strength. He wiggled on the ground like a worm and yelled as he tried to free his arms with all his might. But it didn't do any good. He was stuck.

And so, he lay there limply. But his eyes were like knives. They tried hard to cut into the other boys. But they couldn't. The boys just kept laughing.

And then it happened. One of the boys forced Jordan's mouth wide open. He tried keeping it shut, but it only made things worse. His face began to sting. They were hitting him.

The boy that was on top of him poured water into his mouth. All that couldn't fit ran over like that in a boiling pot. They waited for Jordan to swallow. But he didn't swallow. He closed his mouth, formed an O-shape, and squirted it in the boys' faces.

This made *them* angry. Before Jordan could figure out what was happening, his coat and shirt were torn off. His shoes were stolen. He was shivering.

It all happened so fast. He was now red all over. And he felt dizzy. The world seemed sideways. While all this went on, he noticed a sharp difference in the air. It was like he was lying on ice all of a sudden. And though his vision seemed to come and go, he did notice something within the wood. It was black and slender. Like a shadow of some sort. And it was behind the boys. Coming closer.

He heard screams. He didn't like those sounds. Not even from those boys who clearly hurt him. But those sounds died away quickly.

Were they gone? Jordan didn't dare move until he felt sure he was alone. That they were far, far away. Or at least, unable to follow him. Then, he tried to stand. That was an event all its own. He kept falling down. But every time he did, he went back on his feet. This happened for a few minutes. Eventually, he found his footing. The cold wrapped around him as if it was strangling him.

The trees were harder to see now. It got darker with every step. Darker and colder. This went on for a long time. At one point, Jordan felt as though he could not go on. His legs seemed to stiffen. His hands were far colder than his mother's now. And his mind was foggier. It made it harder to think and to make decisions.

He was about to collapse in the darkness, allowing the biting wind to overtake him. But just as he was about to let himself fall, his feet came across something wet. But it wasn't only wet. It was warm. *Very* warm.

PART II
THE WATERS

He was standing in some kind of shallow wellspring. Or maybe it was a stream. Whatever it was, even with his feet in, his body felt much warmer. His legs began to relax. The muscles felt more free to move. Even his fingers were able to tap and dance at will.

Jordan kept walking forward into the water. It finally came to about his knees, which was good enough for him to just plunge right in. Boy, did it feel good. Not only that, but it smelled like sweet peas. The kind that climbed his mother's lattice near the garden in the summertime. He loved that smell.

It was still dark, and he could hardly make out

any trees. But he didn't care. Not now, at least. He went under, letting the water rise above his head. And for a moment, he thought he saw the water glow. Jordan opened his eyes. It was so clear that he could see all the little fish. *Fish?* If he could see the fish, that meant there was some kind of light!

He bobbed his head out of the water. The darkness that seemed to surround him just moments ago was no longer pressing on him. The woods finally opened up. The sun poked through the yellow leaves. And it was no longer cold. But maybe that was because he was still in this warm stream.

And that was what it was. A stream. Because there was light again, Jordan saw it bent through the wood in different directions. The water flowed gently along. Everything felt calm.

Everything, including his own body. His head stopped pounding. The dizziness went away. And looking at his arms and legs and feet, all that blood seemed to have disappeared. Those large wounds that the boys made were gone. It was as if he never met them at all.

The current moved peacefully. But it *was*

moving. It was as if it had somewhere to go. Someone to see. So Jordan decided to follow. He didn't know why, but he did not seem so concerned about the boys or the townspeople or even his mother. This place, whatever it was, seemed to make all his troubles, his concerns, and his fears melt away. He didn't care that he was unsure of where he was. He didn't seem lost, even though this place felt unfamiliar. He had clearly never been here before. But that was okay. At least, that's how Jordan felt about it.

He began to walk in the stream when confusion rested on him. He hadn't thought about it until now, but he was going up. Up and up. Taking a good look at his surroundings, he'd say he was moving toward the top of a hill. And so was the current. Not down like it was supposed to. Like all the other streams he had played in before, and he had played in many. So he was pretty sure this was strange.

But on he went. The water was warm. His body felt as good as ever. And just before he reached the top, Jordan began to hear whispers. It sounded sweet and kind. Maybe those whispers weren't whispers at all. Perhaps it was a song. A song being sung just for him.

He bent down toward the stream. Yes, it was coming from the water itself. His ear nearly touched its surface when he finally realized what it was saying.

"A boy! It's a boy! A boy is here!" the waters sang happily. To Jordan, it sounded as if there were a *dozen* voices. Curious…

The waters leapt over rocks and onto higher ground. The current never slowed. If anything, he felt as if he was being pushed now. Though still with a kind of gentleness, it became so intense that Jordan decided simply to float on his back. Why walk when he could glide?

His mother taught him how to swim. They would hike to a pond near their property. She would hold him kindly in her arms at first. And he would splash and kick and play, feeling completely safe. But over time, she would begin to let go. And then she would stand some distance away. And then, further still. Pretty soon, Jordan would be doing laps on his own. And she would be watching him.

The thought of her being so happy to see him swim made Jordan smile. Oh, if only she could be here with him now. Would she come here if she died…? Was *he* dead? Huh, he didn't seem too worried about it right now.

The colorful leaves above him thinned until what was left was an open blue sky. Now that his ears were entirely underwater, he heard many different melodies. They all had to do with him. Come to think of it, Jordan was unsure if they were singing *to* him. But they were certainly singing *about* him. How a boy had come. A *real* boy! And about a king.

"A boy, is it?" Jordan heard. But it was muffled. Maybe because it was coming from the land, not there in the water.

He lifted his head so his ears could hear properly. And there, he saw many new and strange things. First, he noticed he was no longer in a stream. That stream flowed into a lake. A big lake. And there was a mountain on the far side. He had never seen this mountain before. It was tall and pointed, like a tooth. Or a volcano. The ones he'd see pictured in the books his mother would show him.

And to his left was a wide, open meadow. Much wider than his back home. And much taller, too. It seemed to stretch on forever. And that meadow seemed alive. In fact, Jordan swore he saw people in there. Not *real* people. But *figures* of people. There in the tall grass. Made *from* the grass.

He was right. Those *were* people. And they were talking to themselves. Jordan could tell they were staring, too. Like the townspeople. But *these* people looked kinder. They looked curious. And they were talking about him. About him being a boy. A boy who had come at last. A sign.

"What sign?" Jordan asked.

At first, he regretted that he said anything. His mother wanted him to stay far away from others. Ordered that he not say a word to anyone. But for some reason, he thought this was a bit different. After all, those rules applied to the townspeople. And he was definitely *not* still in town. And if this helped, he felt he could trust the meadow people.

They all seemed surprised that he spoke to them. Not *angry* surprised. But happy that someone like him talked to people like them.

Maybe they *were* real people, Jordan thought. Maybe not every person had to look like him or his mother.

Before the meadow people could speak, Jordan noticed the water begin to move. The surface of the lake rumbled. It reminded Jordan of when he cooked with his mother. How they would heat a large pot of rainwater on the stove for dinner before putting in the hard pasta. And how Jordan would stand there watching it begin to kick and splash. The lake became like that.

In just a few moments, the flat, glassy lake looked to Jordan as if it were dancing. Lines of water leapt from one end of the lake to the other. Other areas shot up as if they were fountains. And the singing. It was clearly heard now.

The boy is here; The boy, at last
The boy through evil wood had passed
And now is here to tell the king
That he would end the water's sting

"But the water *didn't* sting me," Jordan said.

The waters suddenly paused their dancing. And

the meadow people continued looking at him in silence for a while.

Jordan decided to get out of the water and show the meadow people and the waters and whoever else was there how he was healed. As he was walking out, he noticed the air was very warm. The breeze was warm. The dirt under his feet was warm. Jordan liked that.

He began to point to where his wounds used to be. To the places where perfect skin was now laid. There was no scab or scarring at all.

"Not *this* water," said one of the meadow people. "On the other side. Where *you* live."

The other side? Other side of *what*? Jordan had never seen this place, but it must not be too far from home. And from his mother. He wondered if she had been here before. And if so, why she didn't tell him. He would have liked to come and visit.

But he soon learned that no one had ever been here. No *human*, that was. Not until now. Until Jordan. This made him very curious. So, was that why his coming was a sign? If they were expecting a boy for a long time, and he was the first one they ever saw, it made sense that they thought he was that one.

"I'm sorry," Jordan told them sincerely, "but my mother's sick. I need to go back."

Yes. He was glad he said it, because Jordan felt as if he might've stayed otherwise. Now, it was slowly coming back to him. That his mother was waiting for him in bed. And not just for him, but for her medicine…But it was gone. What would he say? How would he get more? He didn't have another slip of paper to hand to the woman in the shop and didn't want to go into town again or see those boys.

"Can you help me?" he asked.

They all looked eager to lend a hand. Jordan told them his situation. As he told the story, he noticed they didn't show great emotion. But at least they looked happy to listen.

"Take this water to her," said another meadow person. "We'll find a flask. We're sure that's all you'll need."

At once, Jordan saw the meadow ripple and wave like the tide. Come to think of it, Jordan had never seen the sea. But his mother told him stories sometimes, and he liked those with the ocean in it.

He remembered how she'd act out the waves, moving her body up and down and using her mouth to make crashing noises. She always made him laugh when she did that.

The meadow stilled. And a meadow person reached their hand out, holding a small flask of dried clay. To some, it probably looked like nothing more than a makeshift bottle. Garbage, maybe. But to Jordan, it was beautiful. Because inside it, it would hold what his mother desperately needed. And if the waters could completely heal *him*, it might do the same for his mother. That bottle held life. He was sure of it.

With the water's encouragement, he ran the flask along the lake's surface. Then, capped it tightly. Out of habit, Jordan moved his hand to place the flask inside his coat, but he had no coat. And no shirt. And no shoes. And *this* place was warm, but now he began to feel that sense of fear again. A sense that was too familiar back home. How was he to make it back in that weather? And how would his mother not worry?

The meadow people saw Jordan's concerned look. It was odd to them because they did not know what to do. Apparently, they had never seen worry before. Maybe because they had never seen a *human* before. And worry, it now seemed clear to Jordan, was unique to humans.

"I'm all right," Jordan said to them as if they had asked. But no one *had* asked, and they were not sure what to make of what he said. Of course, he was all right. They hadn't gotten to know any different. "But I need to go home."

It took a few minutes of conversation for the people to understand what Jordan meant by *home*. To them, home was with *them*. The meadow people and the waters knew that there were *sides* to this world. That was true. But it seemed complicated for them. They couldn't fully understand their differences.

They saw him come from the forest. It was only natural that he would go back in the same direction, so they pointed that way.

There was no grand farewell, which made Jordan a bit sad. He thought there might be. Maybe they assumed he would come back. But it was better this way. He didn't know if he would ever *really* see them again. He had only found this place by chance. And he didn't know where he was. Besides, his mother took first place right now.

Jordan walked against the current, which slowed down so he could easily walk. It was still very warm, a sensation he knew would not be the case once he returned to where he came from.

The meadow was now out of sight, and he was treading down, down, down the wooded hill. Pretty soon, things got dark again. *Real* dark. Just like last time. He paused in the nice, warm water for a while, knowing that when he left it, he would feel cold…

Well, he better get on with it, then. And just as the last of his toes rose out of the water, a pair of glowing green eyes blinked in the middle of the darkness.

PART III
THE SHADOW

Those eyes looked like slits to Jordan. The slits of a snake. He'd encountered snakes here and there over the years. It was only natural since he played outside half the time. But it was only when his mother opened that big textbook of hers that he could see them up close. And that was about the only time he wanted to.

But this was no textbook. These eyes were *real.* And they were glowing. Something he didn't know a snake's eyes could do. And they wouldn't let go of his. This was when Jordan realized his sense of fear came back with great force. But where would he run to? He was in the middle of a darkened forest. And no matter where he stepped now, he could not find the warm waters again.

"Congratulations," a voice called out. It came from the direction of those eyes.

The voice was deep and smooth. It sounded sure. And very calm. A bit different from the biting wind that hissed in his ears.

Jordan asked what the congratulations were for, which made the voice laugh. It wasn't a mean laugh. Not spiteful. It sounded friendly, actually. But the kind of laugh that his mother would make when he asked silly questions.

"Why," the voice said, "for tricking me."

Tricking? That was a word Jordan heard of before. But it wasn't something he ever thought he should be doing. In fact, his mother taught him absolutely *not* to trick. So he felt a bit confused. Maybe also a little put to shame. He didn't like being accused of tricking anybody. But apparently, he was never supposed to find the warm waters. Or what lay beyond it. That's what the voice told him. But somehow, Jordan had done so.

Jordan had many questions in his head and wondered which one he should ask first…Well, he really wanted to be able to see this snake. For all he knew, it could be a big one. And seeing that the eyes were high in the air, maybe five or six feet off the ground, Jordan guessed this snake *was* giant. Perhaps bigger than he even wanted to imagine.

"Oh, but that's the point," said the voice. "I don't want anyone to see me."

What a strange thing to say, Jordan thought. It made itself known well enough. Jordan saw those piercing green slits. Heard its silky voice. Not to mention, it approached *him*. Not the other way around. Why *wouldn't* this snake want to be seen?

"Ah, but *I* see *you*," it continued. "And that's what really matters."

By the sound of it, Jordan wondered if the thing behind those eyes was smiling. Maybe it was. He didn't know if he liked that.

Then, the snake, or whatever it was that spoke to Jordan, said something that made his eyes widen. Yes, it was a shock to Jordan that it told him his name. And he hadn't mentioned it himself yet. It somehow *knew*...But the shadowy snake sounded kind enough. Laughed it off as if it was expecting Jordan to feel a bit surprised.

"And I knew your father, too," it went on. And

it told Jordan of a time, years ago — seven to be exact — when a man, his father, came to visit.

"Oh, I would consider him an old friend," the snake said as if thinking about the memory as it spoke.

Jordan leaned in with begging ears. He realized he had a lot to learn about his father. His mother had always seemed to keep him and those old days to herself. And Jordan had never thought to ask. Of course, the two would talk about his father from time to time. They would make sentimental statements like "I miss him," and "he always loved you, you know," and things like that. But now, beginning to hear the snake's story, Jordan began to understand that he didn't really know him at all. And that made him sad.

"Yes, he had come to visit once," said the snake. "He knew where to find me. He knew I would help him."

Help him? What could his father possibly want help with? How did he even know where to find this shadowy snake? Jordan just happened to cross paths with it. Or, at least, that's how it appeared to him.

The shadowy voice sounded deeper in thought now. It told of how his father was sick. *Really* sick. This made Jordan think of his mother. Of her cold, cold hands. Was that how his father died? Just like his mother? *Cold?* Or did he not die since he got help?

Jordan found out that the whole town was made sick by its waters. It trapped them there. Killed them there. "Oh, yes, very sick," the snake assured Jordan when he seemed confused. "And it was your father's time to…*you know*…So he found me."

Apparently, everyone knew about the shadowy snake. But it was much harder for people to find it. No one knew where it lived. "I'm a shadow, you see," it said.

So it *wasn't* a snake. Just a shadow? But those eyes…

The shadow — *Snake? Man?* — only showed itself when someone needed help. "And that's why you tricked me," said the shadow man. "You were dying, and you found the stream before you asked me for help."

"I was supposed to ask?" Jordan questioned.

"Yes, of course," said the shadow man.

Jordan had no idea about the stream or about the shadow man. So how could he have asked? But he didn't say this out loud. Instead, he decided to continue listening to the shadow man's story.

"Your father was on the verge of dying, too," it went on.

Not dying like Jordan had been after those boys had gotten to him. But dying, as he thought, like his mother. From the inside. Slow. Painful. And cold.

"Yes, on the very brink," it said. "And there he was begging that I let him drink."

The stream. That's where Jordan's father was desperately trying to go. But no one, absolutely no one, could go to the stream unless they went to the place where the shadow man hid. A place no one really knew about. And after all that, *if* they could find it, they had to fall down on their knees and plead. They had to beg for the shadow man to let them through.

"One drop was all he needed," it said. "That revived him."

At that very moment, Jordan's heart swelled

with hope. His father. *Alive*...But if he was alive, where was he? Jordan told the shadow man that he hadn't seen his father in seven years. There was a distinct sadness in the boy's eyes and in his voice as if he was reliving the tragic news about his father all over again.

"Oh, but he didn't *die*," it affirmed. "He did the only reasonable thing to escape the poisoned waters. He left town."

Left town? So when Jordan's mother would say that his father got lost in the woods, was that what she meant? Did she know? He thought she meant dead because of how she looked — with those shiny eyes and red nose — and by the way she used to talk about him. But Jordan then realized that maybe being left behind was just as painful.

Another thought came into Jordan's mind: If they were all affected by the waters, and if his father found that healing stream, this would mean he left his family to die here.

Anger boiled up inside him. It was a feeling he rarely felt. And never this hard. Jordan's fists tightened without thought. He tasted blood on his lip. He must have bitten down hard. And though it was pitch black, the shadow man must have been able to see Jordan's red face.

"Don't be so upset," it said in a soothing voice. But Jordan didn't feel very soothed. "Look what you have here. In your hand. The very waters that practically brought him back to life."

That was true. But Jordan didn't care about that now. Not *yet.* It was challenging to think about anything and anyone but his father right now. How his father left his mother to die. And how that meant he was left to carry on alone. What if Jordan never found the waters? That only made his bitter thoughts run colder.

And the shadow man considered his father a *friend?* "I consider all those I help to be my friend," it said defensively. "Won't you forgive him?"

Forgive? Jordan had heard that word before. It was one of his mother's favorite words. But it seemed hard to understand now, given what he just learned about his father. *Forgive.* Jordan realized that word was not as simple as he had come to believe.

"Or better yet," said the shadow man, "avenge

your mother. Give her this water. Do what your father wouldn't do."

Yes, the shadow man was right. His mother's well-being would make this wrongful situation better. In some ways. At least, it would make Jordan feel less crummy.

Maybe this shadow man was not so scary after all. Even though it let his father get away, it appeared that it was also going to let *him* go, too.

"My gift to you," said the shadow man. Though Jordan still could not see anything, he felt cold hands wrap around his own. The hands that were cupping the flask of healing waters. "For tricking me."

Jordan's heart felt a little bit lighter now. He was going to be allowed to keep the flask.

"But," the shadow man stopped Jordan in mid-thought, "I have one condition."

A condition? Jordan had also heard of that word. But that was only used when he had to make deals with his mother about getting to play outside. It also involved cleaning up or studying afterward as a form of payment. A compromise.

Jordan was bracing himself for the not-so-good

condition. He wondered if it would be worth keeping the flask...*Of course,* Jordan thought immediately. Anything to save his mother.

"If she gets sick again," it said slowly, "make sure you come back *together.*"

That was it? Come back and get help? He liked that condition. In fact, it didn't even seem like a condition at all. Yes, Jordan was sure. He liked the shadow man very much now.

"Just ask next time," it added. Jordan could sense it smiling. He couldn't help but smile back.

Then, within a few moments, the biting wind picked up. And the darkness began to fade like a large patch of fog sliding away. It was still cold, but at least he could see the woods around him again. As he suspected, Jordan wasn't near the stream anymore. In fact, there wasn't a stream in sight. It was as if he had walked far away from it, even though he was sure he only took a few steps.

Anyway, the shadow man with those green slits for eyes was gone now. When Jordan called out to it, it didn't answer. And in his hands was that flask made of clay. Feeling the rough, hard edges reminded him of his mission. His mother. He needed to get back to his mother.

Jordan didn't know which direction to run in. He was utterly confused. But he couldn't just stand there, so he started moving his feet. He remembered that he had to go down to get the medicine. That meant that his journey home was upward. So he went in the direction where the wood began to climb.

It took a while. Maybe an hour. At first, Jordan felt discouraged. He thought he was going in the opposite direction. But then, the trees around him began to look familiar. Eventually, he noticed the makeshift fort he had once made of twigs and dried-up leaves. He was getting closer.

The sun was now sparkling faintly through the tops of the trees when he finally stepped out into a clearing. It was a meadow. *His* meadow. Jordan ran full speed through it. His sight was focused entirely on the house in the distance. His mind on one thought: his mother.

He shoved the door open and scrambled inside. It was cold. The fire he stoked before he left was completely out now. And his mother. She was still there in bed. But her face was very pale. The color of ice. Even with the distance between them, Jordan could see that.

"Mama!" he exclaimed as he ran over to her.

Her eyes were shut, her lips dark blue. When Jordan tried to shake her awake, it felt like he was shaking a statue.

But to his relief, she opened her eyes. At first, it was a weak try. Then, the eyes gave way to surprise. They widened even more as she began to process who was kneeling down beside her. It was her son, Jordan. And he had a flask with him.

But she didn't notice that. She only saw *him*. Shirtless, shoeless Jordan. He could tell she looked sad by the way her face tightened.

He called her name again. This time, it was gentle. It was kind. And he was expecting the same type of response. But his mother's words didn't sound kind. And it was far from gentle.

"Where were you!?" she shouted. She was so weak that her head was still on her pillow. But Jordan was sure she was very upset. He rarely experienced an outburst. Almost never. And now, with the healing waters in his hands, he definitely wasn't expecting *this*.

Jordan tried to tell his mother where he was. He didn't understand. It had only been a few hours. They had talked about him taking that long. She knew he probably would come back around sunset. And it was now sunset. What could have been the problem?

"You've been gone for a whole day!" she screamed. "A whole day where I thought you were dead!"

His mother was yelling with tears in her eyes. Jordan's eyes couldn't help but fill up with tears, too. He had never heard his mother in such rage before. Such fearful, dreadful rage. But he had never been thought dead before, either. So it was a new experience for both of them. And both of them didn't want to experience this moment again.

Before he could explain himself, he was asked if he drank the water. "No," he said, which seemed to stop her hot, pressing anger. In fact, his mother's tense expression almost entirely washed away after that answer.

He did look completely unharmed. After the healing waters, his encounter with the boys seemed as if it never happened. Jordan decided he probably didn't have to mention that part to her. He didn't want to see that worried face again.

Even though his mother spoke harshly, he could hear in her voice that she was fading away quickly. Then, he remembered. He'd been gone a whole day! Could his mother be telling the truth? Of course. She was his mother. He had no reason not to trust her. And by her sudden panic attack, he could tell her words were severe. But a *whole day*...Jordan wondered for a moment.

It must have been his time on that other side. Beyond the stream. To him, it felt like he was there for only an hour. But time may have moved differently there. By the looks of it now, that world must have moved slower than the time spent here on this side.

And if he'd been gone a day, then his mother spent a day in bed. A day without him there. A day without food. A day without medicine.

Jordan had to act now. Without giving any more thought to it, he lifted the flask onto the bed. His mother glanced at it.

"Water," he said.

"*Water?*" His mother suddenly seemed worried again. But why? She was used to drinking all kinds of water…even poisonous water.

"These waters heal, Mama," he said.

It was odd. Jordan noticed his mother's eyes widen in wonder. Maybe in disbelief. But it clearly looked as if she knew what he was talking about. *Is it really?* He could sense she was asking him that question by the way she eagerly stared at it. At that dull, handmade flask.

He unscrewed the bottle. The smell of sweet peas. Yep. It was definitely the waters from that stream. So he lifted up his mother's head. She craned her neck so that she could drink all right.

But once the waters touched her lips, her face began to scrunch up in an ugly way. Then, she spit it right onto the floor.

Jordan stared at his mother with heavy confusion. These were the *healing waters*. They healed *his body*. They healed his father. Of course, they would heal his mother.

They tried a second time. She seemed a bit reluctant, but she craned her neck anyway. Again, she spit it right out.

"That's awful!" she exclaimed.

Awful? Jordan had to try it himself. With doubt now seizing his heart, he leaned his head back and tried to chug the rest.

But he couldn't do it. Once it touched his lips, it tasted so brilliantly disgusting that he willingly let it spill down his bare chest. Sitting there in hopeless disbelief, he thought about how right his mother was. It was like eating rotten trash that was lying waste for a few days. Or like licking the stuff that he would vomit up at night. Or like a toilet bowl that hadn't been flushed. Yes, it was that bad.

He gave his mother a fearful glance. What were they going to do now? He didn't tell her yet about the lost medicine. And now, what he thought was the source of hope was sprayed all over their floor.

What could this mean? Had the shadow man tricked him? But no one had touched the flask except him. Jordan drew the waters out himself. Did the shadow man somehow switch the healing waters for the poisonous ones? And make it smell nice so he wouldn't suspect anything?

Jordan grabbed onto his mother's hand with a mixture of longing and despair. *Extremely* cold.

And brittle. Very brittle. This was it. This was her end. And he would be alone. His body began to shake with the thought.

But then, he remembered what the shadow man said. His condition. Somehow, it knew this might happen. Thankfully, Jordan could go back, and it would help her. Help them both.

With a deep breath, Jordan rose from the floor and began tugging on his mother's hand.

PART IV
THE BOY

She didn't budge. Jordan tugged harder. It was no use. So he began to plead with her to get up. Those blue eyes of hers were hidden behind sunken eyelids. And he noticed that they were no longer as warm.

"Mama, please," he whimpered.

"Go," she said. At first, Jordan wondered if she meant for him to get help. But as he was about to turn on his heel, his mother added, "Leave."

Leave...Like his father? Just abandon her?

"You're not cursed," she heaved. It was clear that she was struggling with every breath. "You never drank the water."

That's right. He never drank the poisoned tap.

You'll die, Jordan again remembered that stern warning. To help him better understand, she finally told him why this was big. Because he never drank the town's water, he was not bound to stay there. He didn't crave the water. He could leave. He could *live*.

But where would Jordan live? This was his home. *She* was his life. His everything. It was hard enough to watch her slip into coldness. How could he, at this most crucial moment, just walk away? Even if it *was* hopeless. He would never be able to forgive himself if he turned his back while she was still alive. His heart would feel forever cold if he up and left right now.

Yes, he would have to journey on once her eyes closed for good. After he huddled close to her frozen body and wept hot tears. He would not be able to stay here. Not when he knew the town that kept his mother there longed to take him also. No, he had to go.

But not yet. Not when Jordan knew her eyes still had a warmth to them.

"I'm not asking you," she said. The words sounded dark to Jordan. They were severe and grim words.

His heart pounded loudly. He didn't want to hear it. He didn't want to listen. And he had *always* listened to his mother. Jordan's mind was heavily conflicted.

"No," Jordan told her with a firm voice.

This surprised his mother. He had never said 'no' to her before, except when he was really small. Since then, he has learned right from wrong. Still, her son said 'no'. She was speechless.

Jordan's eyes were fierce and determined. She could see that. To her, those eyes were different. *He* was different.

"Okay," she whispered.

That one simple word meant the world to Jordan. It meant that there was still a chance. His mother smiled at him. It was weak, terribly weak. But it was a smile that trusted him. He smiled back.

Then, he told her she needed to get up. They needed to go into the woods and find that stream. He didn't tell her he made a deal with the shadow man.

It was hard for Jordan to get his mother to

understand that he had found the waters. And it was even harder to get her to sit up. But she seemed willing. Her body, though. It was failing her. Quickly.

Food, Jordan realized. She hadn't eaten in over a day! He rushed into the kitchen. Along the back wall of the pantry sat the last can of chicken noodle soup. The only thing left in that cupboard.

He turned on the stove. And instead of filling the pot with tap water, he drew rainwater from one of their many basins. He wasn't going to let his mother drink any more of that poison! Not if he could help it.

His mother insisted that Jordan share the bowl of soup. Again, Jordan refused. She looked sad as she ate it herself. Maybe it was hard for her to see the change in her son. Now older. Stronger. No longer the little boy who left their home for the first time to get medicine. In just a day, he had somehow become a man. It happened all too fast.

Jordan felt grateful when the soup seemed to do some good. His mother was able to stand up. She rocked at first, which made him worry. He didn't want her to fall over and make matters worse. But she was able to adjust. He made sure to keep a hold of her the whole time.

Jordan wrapped his mother up as much as possible. Two layers of socks. Three undershirts. An oversized winter coat. A woolen scarf. Mittens. Earmuffs. Everything a cold, dying woman would need to brace the outside.

It was slow going. The journey felt more like a heavy shuffle than a light walk in the woods. Jordan's mother leaned on him for support at every step. He wasn't taller than her yet. This made it a bit more challenging to steady and guide her. But he did it anyway. And with his free arm, he pointed a flashlight ahead of them.

It was dark tonight. Darker than usual. The moon wasn't out. But all the nighttime animals were. Owls. Cats. And other things…

His mother stopped at one point. She was tired. Weak. "I can't go on," she said. "I'm sorry."

He refused this, too. And with some encouragement, Jordan got his mother to shuffle again.

He really did feel bad. He could tell her legs were stiff. So were her arms and the rest of her body. Each step must have been painful for her. But Jordan didn't want to think about that. Her constant whimpers didn't help.

Eventually, he spun the flashlight around. Where were they? He began to feel lost. Maybe this wasn't a good idea. Maybe they should have waited until morning.

No. Jordan couldn't have waited any longer. This was his only option.

And now, after spending hours in the woods, he was about to collapse. His mother's weight felt heavier on him. It could have been because she put more of herself on his body. Or it could be that he was getting tired himself. It was probably both.

But that was it. He was done. His strength was gone. Jordan struggled to lean his mother against a tree. He sat next to her, feeling like jelly. The stuff his mother would make for dessert sometimes. He loved how it tasted but didn't like how it felt right now.

After a moment or two, Jordan stumbled back to his feet. He pointed his flashlight at his surroundings. The woods seemed to go on forever.

Well, he might as well try… "Mr. Shadow

Man!" Jordan called out. He just now thought about it. He didn't know its name.

A scare came when his mother quickly grabbed his arm. He wasn't expecting that. When he looked over at her, he noticed those blue eyes were wide. Fear was inside them. "What are you doing!?" she whispered. More harshness. Would Jordan ever hear her gentle voice again?

"Getting help," Jordan replied.

It looked as if his mother knew who he was calling. Then, he remembered the shadow man telling him how the town knew about it. But his mother didn't seem happy that he was calling the shadow man. Her unhappiness made him uneasy. Little, chilled bumps began to crawl up his arm.

Then, they were there. Those green slits for eyes. In the distance. Not too far away. *Glowing.* Jordan flashed his light on it. And there, he could see its form. It was tall and thin, like a man. But it *was* a shadow. Jordan couldn't sense any depth or light to it.

It walked between the trees. Closer. Closer. His mother let out a shiver as it reached them. The shadow man said hello to Jordan. By name. "And I see your mother is here with you...I'm sorry she continues to be unwell."

Was that true? Jordan wanted to believe its words, but something told him they were lies. And lying, he had learned from his mother, was one of the worst things a person could ever do.

It was his mother's fear-filled eyes that helped Jordan understand. They kept flashing in his head, even though he was now looking at the shadow man. But it was too late.

"W-we need help," said Jordan to the shadow man. "M-my mom is d-dying."

"I see," it said smoothly. Always so smooth.

Jordan reminded the shadow man of what it said earlier that day. That it would help them if he asked. But even as he said those words, he doubted them. He doubted the shadow man now more than ever.

"I must apologize," it said, sounding just as calm. "You deserve to know that I don't always tell the truth."

And that's when it happened. Jordan saw those green slits become sharp and pointed. They looked mean. But happy, too. Then, the shadow man's body swooped over them. And she was gone. Darkness separated them.

Jordan couldn't stand to hear his mother scream like that. He didn't know if she was crying out for her life or for his. The sound quickly died away, but it echoed in his mind for a long time.

Jordan began to stumble forward, trying to escape. But there was no escape. His flashlight pointed at black on black. And it was getting colder. Much, *much* colder. The wind whipped him. It brought him to his knees.

"Mama!" he cried.

Jordan couldn't see it, but he could feel it. Snow began to fall in clumps. Then, it felt as if he was being pulled in opposite directions. His body began to move and shift in ways he never thought possible. As if two forces were fighting for his body. For his soul.

The ground under him disappeared. Was he in the air now? The wind slashed harder and harder. Each snowflake was a sting on his face. His ears, those frozen ears, could only hear the biting air. Jordan was being torn apart. All he could do now was let out a long, painful shriek. Then, it was over.

It went black and silent for a long time. A *very* long time. But Jordan didn't experience this. He was gone.

Warmth was the first thing Jordan began to sense. The second was the sound of water. Gentle flowing water. But not under him. Not above or far from him. It sounded as if he was *in* the water. Floating. The third thing he sensed was the smell of sweat peas. Beautiful, delicate sweet peas.

He opened his eyes. The sky was blue. A bright blue, as if the sun was right above him. But there was no sun. Not in *that* sky.

The view was partly hidden by all the tall grass that seemed to lean over him. But it wasn't *just* grass, Jordan saw. It was the meadow people, and they were staring down at him with their curious grass-like eyes. He was back in that place, somehow. In that healing stream. On the other side. In another world entirely.

No one spoke at first. The waters that he was in didn't even hum. They all let the boy take in his surroundings. When he fully realized that he was floating in the healing waters, Jordan sat up. The current was shallow enough for him to find a comfortable spot on the rocks and still easily have his head poking out. He liked that.

Jordan didn't know how he got there. Didn't know why. Didn't have any thoughts beyond the scene he was in right now. And it was calm and peaceful.

He blinked a few times. That was when the meadow people finally started talking to each other. They all seemed excited that the human boy was back. Jordan asked how long he had been away. "Only a minute or two," answered one of them.

A minute or two? So, to them, he never really left. He did remember saying goodbye to them. He sensed that he had been gone for a while. But Jordan couldn't seem to place what happened. The time between then and now was lost to him.

He didn't care. He was here. That's what mattered. At least, that's how Jordan felt about it.

And then he heard a familiar tune. The waters began to echo it.

The boy is here; The boy, at last
The boy through evil wood had passed
And now is here to tell the king
That he would end the water's sting

Yes, he had heard this song before. It was about him. *He* was that boy. And for some reason, he had to tell the king something very important.

As Jordan was thinking about the lyrics, one of the meadow people asked him about the flask. *A flask*…He did remember something about a flask.

"Did you give it to your mother?" they asked.

Mother…His mother! Yes, it was flooding in now. Like a broken basin. All the memories came rushing back. Jordan's flask of healing waters. His encounter with the shadow man. The shadow man's promise to help his dying mother. The healing waters tasting foul. Their journey into the woods. *That betrayal*…His mother was gone. Dead. Well, maybe. Jordan wasn't sure. But it seemed that way. That scream she howled was very convincing.

But if she was dead, wasn't he dead, too? Well, Jordan wasn't dead the last time he was here…It was all too confusing for him.

Now that the memories returned, so did his fear. So did his intense sadness, anger, and hopelessness. All these feelings seemed new for the meadow people to see. They simply stared at Jordan as he splashed around and took short breaths. They must have been able to experience feelings, but it was clear to Jordan they had never experienced those. His tears were also new to them. Had they never seen a boy cry?

The boy is here, the boy at last! The boy through evil wood had passed. And now is here to tell the king that he would end the water's sting. Jordan wasn't sure what this king was. He knew nothing about him. But he knew that his next steps were to go to that king. And he had to tell him about the water. About the poison. Somehow, this was going to help stop it.

"How?" Jordan asked the waters. If they sang about it, they must have known more.

And they did. They continued in song. Apparently, there was more to it than what they first sang.

He would by flesh to them return
To then confront the dark cistern
By blood so pure a drop would do
And make the dirty waters new

Jordan had the waters repeat the stanza a few times. To really soak it in. Was this what he had to do to save his mother? *Die*, so she could live? Was she even alive?

Some things were clearer than others. He was the pure one. The only one kept safe from the poisoned tap all these years. The only one who stumbled across this strange place. He was the one to tell the king. And he finally knew what it was he had to say to him.

"I'm going to die," Jordan said under his breath. "For my mother."

It took only a few moments to think it over. Yes, he was ready. He had by now gone this far for her. He risked it all. Of course, there used to be that slight chance that both of them could live...

That wasn't possible anymore. But he didn't care. He didn't care about his life. Not as much as he cared about his mother's. Hopefully, she was still able to be saved. If death was what it took, he would take it. If this was how far he needed to go, he would go the distance.

Jordan breathed in and made himself steady. Then, he kindly asked the waters to take him to the king.

PART V
THE KING

Where the water rises. That's what the waters told him. That's where he would find the king. And they were happy to lead him there. But when Jordan stood up, the world looked dizzy. His head felt lighter. He was hungry. *Really* hungry. The boy hadn't eaten since yesterday.

The meadow people asked what the matter was. Jordan told them. Thankfully, the people on this side of the world ate. He wasn't sure if they did at first. After all, the people were made of grass. And Jordan couldn't explain how the waters were even alive. But if they had food, he wanted it. *Bad.*

He was told to sit by the lake. So he got out, walked a short way, and sat down. Some meadow people helped him. The same way *he* had helped his mother in the woods. Jordan dipped his toes in the warm waters. He could feel the living waters playing with them. He liked that. It reminded him of when his mother used to give him baths. She would play with his toes. Tell the same old story about some piggy going to market and another staying home.

Soon enough, a meadow person returned from the tall grass. It held a clay bowl. And what was in that bowl didn't look like food at all. Not to Jordan. There were small twigs and crushed-up leaves and two acorns. This made his stomach growl even louder. He made a note to himself not to ask them for food again.

No one seemed upset that Jordan turned the bowl away. They could tell he still seemed hungry, so the waters invited him to drink from the lake. "Drink us down!" they chirped. "And want no more!"

That's right! Why didn't he think of that? But just as he bent over the edge to drink, Jordan paused. He remembered how the waters didn't help his mother. How it tasted foul to them both.

But all the meadow people were watching him. He sensed the waters waiting, too.

Slowly, Jordan bent his tongue into the waters. The moment it touched the surface, it felt as if the awful flavor went through his entire body. He fell back onto the ground.

All those around him looked confused. Jordan felt confused, too. And he told that to the waters. "But you healed me before. Why can't I drink it?"

"I don't know, I don't know," the waters quickly said one by one.

But the waters didn't sound worried. Again, Jordan learned worry was a purely human response. No, they seemed intrigued. Curious. But Jordan felt scared. Why would they heal his wounds but taste too bad to swallow? No one had an answer for him.

"The Water King would know," said a meadow person.

The Water King. So that was his title... Was this the king he meant to talk to? Yes, it seemed to be. It was fitting that the one who lived "where the water rises" would be called the Water King. But did he just rule the waters? Or did he also rule this side of the world? Maybe he ruled Jordan's world, too.

His thoughts were few. His lack of food outweighed any other thing right now. But he felt well rested, at least. Jordan's little nap seemed to help.

But was it a little nap? How long was he out for? Every moment counted here. Jordan began to feel restless. How could he sit by the bank, dipping his toes in the water, when his mother was gone? If she was not dead by now, she would be soon. Time moved differently here. How much time has he wasted already? A day? A week?

"How long was I asleep for?" Jordan asked those around him.

Another confusing question for them. Why were they so lost? Have they never heard of time?

Well, maybe not. Maybe the meadow people and the living waters and everything else on this side did not understand time. Or, at least, did not care about it. This made Jordan's lips tighten and his forehead tense up. If they didn't care or even understand time, how would they be able to help him?

There was a word his mother had taught him, and it seemed to work well here. The word was *urgency*. A word this world clearly lacked.

Jordan eventually relaxed. How could he get so worked up? He never used to care about time, either. It wasn't until his mother got sick that time seemed to exist at all for him. He couldn't really be too judgmental of these people. It wouldn't be fair. After all, they kept him alive.

The landscape began to tilt again when Jordan went back on his feet. Nope. He needed to eat. *Now*. It was that or get stuck lying on the ground forever. "I need real food," Jordan told the meadow people as he sat back down. "Or I can't go to the king."

These chosen words helped the meadow people understand his trouble a little bit better. *No food. No message.* So they needed to give him food. But what was real food? To them, it was twigs and leaves and acorns.

"Meat," Jordan said. And he told them what meat was. It was clear from their faces that what he was asking for was impossible.

Okay, so no meat. "How about potatoes?" Yes,

they knew what potatoes were. A few meadow people disappeared into the tall grass again.

Time passed. Jordan waited. He had no strength left except to lay his head down and stare at the bright, blue, sunless sky. At least he was warm, here, in this place.

"Does it ever get dark?" he asked at one point.

No, apparently not. There were no nights, he was told. And if there were no nights, there were no days.

Jordan thought about that for a little bit. But it soon flew away when a bowl of potatoes was placed beside him. They were freshly picked, he could tell, since they were still covered in dirt.

With permission, he washed the potatoes in the waters and dried them off with his shirt. Then, he bit into them. Jordan had never eaten a raw potato before. But wow, did it taste better than he imagined. Honestly, it didn't remind him of a potato at all. They definitely looked and felt like potatoes. But the flavor was sweet, like corn. And it was buttery, like bread. This made him reconsider trying the twigs, leaves, and acorns. But he eventually decided against this.

The nine or ten fist-sized potatoes were gone in no time. Then, Jordan jumped to his feet. Yes, his strength was coming back in full force. His vision was all steady now. His thoughts felt clearer. He was ready to see the king.

"Follow us," said the waters. "Beyond the lake. Follow us into the mountain. You'll find him there."

Jordan saw that the lake had a few offshoots. One where water entered from the woods. The same woods he came from. And then, on the other side of the lake, there was a stream that left for the mountain. To that pointed, toothy place.

He swam over to the other side. The water felt light and easy to cut through. Jordan realized he probably couldn't sink here even if he tried. But he didn't test this theory.

The stream near the base of the mountain was rocky. Jordan made sure to watch his footing. While it didn't wind into a forest, the stream twisted through a scene of all kinds of plants and trees. He noticed that some of them had apples on them. He plucked a few. They were the best he ever had.

On his way, Jordan remembered that he didn't say goodbye to the meadow people. But then he also remembered that they didn't understand goodbyes, so he didn't feel so bad this time. And the waters…Well, they were right there with him. Humming and stirring around his ankles. *The boy is here; the boy, at last,* the waters kept on whispering in song.

As the ground became steeper, so did the waters. Climbing the mountainside was not daunting for the stream. But Jordan had to admit it was a little bit for him. He had never gone hiking with his mother. *His mother*…The simple thought of her made his strength come back in full.

After a little while, the ground became too sharp for the plants and trees. So, Jordan found himself on an open slope. The stream twisted higher and higher toward the top. And he saw the lake and the meadow and the woods below. What a view! But he didn't stop for long. Jordan pressed on. For his mother. And maybe because he was a bit afraid of heights, too.

The walk eventually turned into a crawl. Yes,

the incline was that steep. Jordan had to use his hands now. But the waters helped him. They pushed him up when he couldn't reach the next boulder. And they wouldn't let him fall back if he slipped. Jordan was safe. He was happy about that.

There was a big opening just ahead of him now. It was near the top of the pointed mountain. A cave of sorts. Jordan had been in a cave once. His mother found a very small one near the pond they used to swim in. It was no bigger than their tiny bathroom, but it was a good enough size for them to eat their packed lunches together.

Jordan hoped all this trouble meant good for his mother. But he couldn't really know that. Still, he hoped.

Thankfully, the stream leveled off as he arrived at the entrance. And it was huge. His house could easily fit inside.

Jordan's eyes opened wider now. His mouth, too. Caves, naturally, are dark. But this one wasn't. The waters were glowing inside. This made its walls and the ceiling reflect the watery light. If this was where the Water King lived, Jordan wanted to be there with him. It looked as grand as a palace.

Like the pictures he'd see in children's books. The ones his mother used to read to him. This one, of course, was a different type of palace. It wasn't a home built by hand. It was a naturally holed-out rock.

There were many paths in this cave. The glowing stream broke off into different passageways. Some left. Some right. But the widest one flowed straight ahead. This seemed the likeliest path to take, Jordan thought. The waters began to dance and sing as he approached a large opening.

It was a hall of sorts. Round and tall. Very tall. The stream he was in flowed toward the center of the room. In fact, many streams entered from all around. They all met in the middle.

The center was the oddest place Jordan had seen so far. The waters were circling around and around. And the circle was raining. It looked kind of like a spiraling waterfall. But it wasn't a waterfall because it wasn't falling. It was *rising*. The waters were falling upward toward an opening above. An opening that led to the sky.

Everything became quieter as he traveled closer

to it. The watery hums began to die away. Soon, all Jordan heard was the flowing waters under him and that strange waterfall.

Other than the living waters, he thought that he was all alone. But there, within the large waterfall itself, he saw something move. It was hard to tell at first. But then, Jordan made out a figure. It was tall and strong-looking. This thing was made of water. And there was a sort of watery crown that blended in with the rest of the head.

There were well-defined features on *this* face, unlike the shadow man. Jordan could make out lips, a nose, and a pair of eyes. But they were all watery, like the rest of it. And it was hard to make it out with the spiraling waters around it.

Him, Jordan corrected himself. This must be the *king!* He had never seen a king before. And so, he didn't know exactly what to do. Those in the books his mother would read to him always bowed before kings. So, taking that cue, Jordan slowly bent over.

It was so quiet now. Even the flowing streams and the rushing waterfall fell silent.

"I have a message for the king," said Jordan. He

knew he was speaking to the king himself. He just didn't know what else to say. Jordan was hoping that the king would have spoken first.

And when the Water King did speak, the first thing he said was Jordan's name. Of course, he would know the boy's name. Just like the shadow man…Was this king like the other? Was he someone to be trusted? But what was there to trust? In the end, it was Jordan who was going to die. Meeting the king was just another step closer to his fate.

Now, he didn't know how this was all going to happen. How his fate would affect his mother. Jordan could die, and she could still be on her deathbed. But at least, maybe there was that tiny chance they *would* see each other again… somewhere beyond death.

Jordan opened his mouth to say something. It took a lot of deep breaths to get that far. But then, the king stopped him. "I know why you're here," said the Water King.

Why was Jordan here? To save his mother. Did the Water King know this? Or was he referring to the prophecy? About ending the water's sting?

Hopefully, they were connected.

"I have a message for you, too," said the king. And by that statement, he meant that Jordan had to wait. He had to listen to the king first. To his deep but soft voice.

"You must be hungry," said the king. Was this the message? If so, it was the *perfect* message! Yes, Jordan was very hungry. And *thirsty*.

Jordan nodded his head weakly. At once, the king called out for food and drink to be brought out to him. Some waters responded by flowing the opposite way. Out of the room.

Jordan tapped his thumbs nervously. He only had to stand there briefly before a tray came in. It was riding on a little wave coming toward him. Jordan grabbed hold of it and looked with big eyes. Food. *Real* food. There was meat. And soup. And even a cookie.

The Water King told him to eat. So Jordan did. He sat on the flat, stony ground. He thought maybe the king would start talking, but he just watched.

Jordan didn't feel so scared of the Water King anymore. Maybe he shouldn't have felt this way, but the king did give him food. Enough to really make a difference. The meadow people couldn't seem to do that on their own. And the shadow man gave him nothing at all. Nothing but a promise he didn't keep. And waters that didn't work.

Didn't work...This was a good time to ask, so Jordan tried to clear his throat. "Excuse me."

The Water King gave the boy his full attention. He didn't seem angry that Jordan spoke with food in his mouth. No, the king looked rather pleasant. So Jordan asked the king why the waters here didn't work on his mother. He explained that they healed his body, but neither could drink it. The king did not seem surprised at all.

"These waters can cure the outside, but they cannot cure the inside," the king told him.

Jordan thought about this for a moment. It made sense, but he didn't understand why it had to be that way.

"It wasn't always like that," replied the king.

The Water King told of a time when people like Jordan — *humans* — used to drink freely from his streams. But since the poisoning, the king's waters didn't just stop working for them. The waters that used to bless them became the waters that would now curse them.

"As long as they have the poison in their blood," the king continued, "my streams will only hurt them."

"But *why*?" Jordan asked. *Why couldn't they heal?*

"Good waters cannot mix with bad waters," said the Water King. "If my waters enter their bloodstream, they will attack the bad waters. And that person will be torn apart. For good."

For good? Jordan now seemed a bit glad that his mother had spit the waters back out. Because *torn apart for good* sounded like a very long time.

"But my father drank the waters," said Jordan. "And *he* was healed…"

"No," said the Water King.

No? "He left town," Jordan said. He wondered if he should talk back like this to a king. He definitely didn't learn this from his mother…

"He never left," the king told him.

Jordan sat there for a minute, unable to eat his cookie. His eyebrows curled, and his eyes squinted. His face scrunched up.

The Water King saw Jordan's confusion. He went on to tell the boy that the shadow man had lied to him about his father.

Lie? So his father was still in town? Did he really know the shadow man? The bitterness Jordan felt toward his father now seemed to go away. It was replaced by the intense need to know the truth. He wasn't sure what the truth was anymore.

Jordan stood up, eyes heavy and wet with tears. He felt as if he had been lashed by the wind over and over again. He wasn't sure what to do. Emotions came crashing down on him. The Water King didn't say anything. He watched Jordan huff and puff with anger. But the king spoke eventually.

"I'm sorry you feel this way," said the king. And he sounded honest. Jordan knew honesty. His mother was a great model of such a word. "So many questions you must have."

Yes, it was true. There were so many. *Too* many. But the Water King promised to answer them all. "Be patient. You *will* come to know them. In due course."

This made Jordan feel better. And it made him trust the Water King. He had to. It was either trust the king or trust nobody. And Jordan had felt all alone ever since he left his house to get medicine. He needed someone to trust in.

The king told the boy to follow one of the streams. This would lead Jordan to a pool that he needed to go into.

"And then, come back to me," said the king.

This was an odd request. To dip into a pool and then return. But Jordan knew that he didn't understand everything. It was easier just to accept. So, with a nod, he did.

PART VI
THE PROPHECY

One of the streams began to glow brighter than the rest. This one was the path to take. Jordan was sure of it. So he walked over to the stream and stepped in. The waters began to flow out of the room to a place, the boy hoped, might give him some clear answers.

The Water King watched silently as Jordan walked out of the large, open room and into a small, cramped corridor. The waters, for the first time, went down. Down and down. And Jordan thought maybe he was going to its dungeons.

But it wasn't a dungeon. The room the waters led him to was small like his bedroom. The ceiling was low. And the stream ended right in the archway. When Jordan looked around, he noticed the waters had broken off and crawled along the rocky walls in many directions. Above him was the pool. As if he was hanging upside down right now. Was he? Maybe. Anything was possible at this point.

Anything, except the answers Jordan wanted. Anything, except his mother being healthy again. Even the strange parts of this world did not seem clear-cut. He thought the waters would heal. But apparently *that* was not possible. Not when the poison lived in his mother's veins. Okay, maybe not everything was possible.

One thing that seemed *impossible* was Jordan finding a way to get into that pool. He had never seen one that floated above him. Wouldn't gravity pull him back down?

"Touch it," the waters whispered to him in echoes.

So Jordan did. And when he touched it, he found that the pool above him was pulling him in. *In?* But Jordan couldn't breath underwater! His heart pumped super fast as he was slowly being dragged into it. "No, please!" he shouted. Unable to let go.

Was this how he was going to die? In an upside down pool? Inside the Water King's strange palace? Would this bring his mother back? But Jordan didn't die in those waters. In fact, Jordan realized he could breathe underwater. Or, at least, within this pool. Swimming inside it was effortless. And with the waters glowing, it seemed to him as if he was flying in the sky. It was all very bright and beautiful. It reminded Jordan of his mother's blue eyes. How he wished he could see them now.

There was a voice, calm and sweet. It sounded as if it was coming from all around him. At first, Jordan thought it must be the waters talking. But it wasn't the waters. After a while, the sound became more finite. As if it was coming from a single place just a short distance away. Maybe it wasn't the waters. No, it sounded familiar now. It was his mother's voice.

"Mama!" Jordan called out. But his mother didn't seem to take notice of him.

Soon, the bright blue waters transformed into a scene. Jordan was still floating, but now he was rushing above a meadow. *His* meadow back home.

His mother was running through it. Smiling. Laughing. Her hair was down. He liked that.

And she was wearing a light summer dress. This must mean she was warm. Looking around, the trees were all green. Jordan even felt the warm air pass through him.

At first, he thought his mother was running away from him. But then he noticed someone else. This man was also in the meadow. And he was chasing after her. He was laughing, too.

Jordan watched as his mother let the man catch up to him. He spun her around and kissed her. *His father*. It had to be. Was this where they were right now? No, it didn't seem so. The two looked much younger. They definitely still seemed older than him, but not quite like adults yet. Was this a memory?

The scene quickly changed, and Jordan was hovering over another open meadow. But it wasn't his. This one was on the other side. Where the meadow people lived. There, he could see the lake and the pointed mountain behind it. Jordan remembered being told he was the only human to go there. But, apparently, he wasn't. His parents were there. And so were many other humans. A wedding was taking place.

Meadow people and the living waters were all gathered around. It was the Water King who was giving the ceremony. And the two getting married were his parents. Everyone looked happy. In fact, he never saw his mother that happy in his life. This made him a bit sad, at first. But then it came to him. That life without his father must have been hard on her. How could she smile so brightly again after he was gone?

The scene changed again, and this time, Jordan found himself in the same, small square he was in to get the medicine. The well sat there. But the streets looked bright and cheery. The well itself was overflowing like a fountain. The people had happy faces. It seemed to go against all that Jordan had seen just the other day. But this scene must have taken place a long time ago. Before he was even born.

A crowd gathered around the well. His father was standing on a small platform. In front of them all. He was speaking to them.

"The Water King has given us this town," said

Jordan's father. "And has made sure his rivers run through it. He has made it a place where we are called to drink from his waters. People from everywhere will travel here. And we will welcome them freely."

It seemed to Jordan that he was in charge of the town. He had learned a word for that…*mayor*. Was his father really the mayor of this town? It was clear something had gone very wrong between then and now.

Jordan didn't have to wait long to find out. The scene changed yet again. He was in the woods. His mother was strolling along the same worn path that he and her used to take. She was alone, but not for long. Something appeared from behind a tree. It was a meadow person. His mother didn't look that surprised. She didn't seem concerned, either.

The meadow person spoke. It sounded friendly and smooth. And it kept a smile on its face. Jordan tried understanding the conversation. The meadow person thought his mother looked thirsty. She said she wasn't ever thirsty. Then, it held out a flask. A shiny, glass bottle that held sparkling waters inside.

His mother tried telling the meadow person that she wasn't allowed to drink any waters that weren't from the Water King's streams. But the meadow person said these waters were special. That these waters were usually only reserved for the king himself to drink. And if the king could drink it, so could she.

The scene changed again before Jordan saw what happened next. Then, he saw his father with his mother. They stood in a kitchen. This kitchen was unfamiliar to him. But it seemed like they were in their home.

His father didn't look very happy at his mother. His eyebrows were scrunched up in frustration as she spoke. She was gentle, like Jordan knew her to be. And she held up a flask of water.

"Try it," she said. "Tastes even better than our own."

When his father kept standing there, she drank some of it. To show him. It looked to Jordan as if she was trying to convince him. It didn't look like it was working.

Not at first. But after some back and forth,

Jordan noticed his father's wrinkled forehead begin to fade. His eyes looked more agreeable. Eventually, he took the flask in his hand. He stared into it. Smelled it. Swirled it around. Then, his father also drank it.

The glass shattered on the floor. In an instant, Jordan saw both of his parents begin to choke. There was coughing. There was gasping. There was falling to the floor. Jordan's pulse began to race. He screamed at them, hoping they'd hear him, but they went on without noticing. They couldn't hear him, of course. This was just a memory. No matter how real they looked, and how physically close he was to them.

Jordan turned to see something in the other room. It was the meadow person. Was it hiding? Did his parents know it was there? A strange sight took place. Its grassy body began to fade into blackness. Like a shadow. And its eyes turned into green slits. Like that of a snake. Jordan gasped. *The shadow man.* So it knew his parents. And it tricked them into drinking forbidden water. But it seemed surprised when it turned into a shadow. Into a curse. It was tricked by its own trick.

Before Jordan could figure out all that was going on, the scene changed for a fifth time. He was now high in the air. High above the streets of his town. The trees were all dead now. Not a leaf was on any of them. A large crowd was gathered at the well. The people didn't look happy by the way they seemed to wrestle each other. To Jordan, they didn't act like humans at all. More like animals. *Possessed.* There were shrieks and laughs. But they didn't sound like his mother's. Hers were always kind and soothing. These were more like those boys who had tried to kill him. Mean. Deadly.

Then, Jordan saw something slither through the mob. It was dark. And without a clear form. The shadow man was making its way to the well. But the people…Jordan wondered if they could see it.

Thankfully, Jordan was brought closer to the scene. A group of people, innocent people, were wrapped up by ropes and chains. The fear in their eyes made him believe that they were different from the rest. These prisoners looked into the narrow green slits of the shadow man.

"Please!" exclaimed one of the prisoners. "We just came to drink from the Water King's stream!"

"Didn't you hear?" said the shadow man in his cool voice. "He abandoned this place. Gave the town over to *me*. So you've come to drink *my* water."

"No!" another one shouted.

"Oh," the shadow man said mockingly. "But I want to give you my water. You'll find it so tasteful, you won't ever want to leave."

Jordan saw it. A smile crossed the shadow man's face. Then, just as fast as it took his mother, the prisoners' heads were plunged into large buckets from the well. Forced to drink it in. Or drown.

The scene changed. He was back with his father and mother. Both of them were in their living room. Both of them had wide-eyed faces. Her hand covered her stomach. There was a bump there. Was that *him*? Jordan?

"We need to leave," she said. Her eyes were wet with tears.

"You know we can't," his father replied. "We're trapped."

"I won't let it take him, too!" Her voice cracked as she said it.

His father's face turned scared. But it looked

determined, too. He nodded carefully. As if a plan was being formed in his head.

The next scene Jordan found himself in was familiar. He knew those walls. Those uneven floorboards. He was home. *His* home. And there *he* was. Just a tyke. Held in his mother's arms.

His father looked sick. Cold and pale, just like his mother did these days. His father spoke confidently to her. He said that he would be back. That everything would be okay. But she was overcome with grief. Jordan could tell that his father was about to leave. This must have been their last goodbye. His mother's red eyes seemed sure of it. Did she know he wasn't coming back?

With one last hug and a kiss to both his mother and little Jordan, his father went out the door. When it shut behind him, she broke down crying. Jordan could see his little self petting her cheeks. Trying to cheer her up. But she wouldn't cheer up.

The scene changed. It didn't seem like much time had passed. Jordan was in the woods now, and he saw his father bundled in the same outfit that he had left the house in. The shadow man appeared in front of him. Jordan wanted to shout and warn his father, but he knew it would do no good. Even though he knew this was a memory, Jordan felt completely helpless. This made him sad. And angry, too.

His father walked away from the shadow man. But it followed him. It asked him what he was doing. "Saving my family," he said to it. He was going to find the Water King's stream.

"But he hid it from you," said the shadow man. "So you would never find it."

"He promised it will be found one day," his father said with confidence.

"Those were just lies," it replied. "He sent me here to take you somewhere else."

His father looked up and asked where to.

"The End," the shadow man said. And Jordan knew those eyes. In a moment, the whole area around his father was wrapped in darkness. His father screamed. And that was it.

The next scene opened up, and it was a very strange one. The sky was dim. Like it barely had any light at all. The whole scene had a red shade to it, even as clumps of snow came down. Jordan was flying over the cold landscape. Bodies lay everywhere. Cold, lifeless bodies. Then, everything turned to shadow. First, the people faded. Then, the landscape. Last of all, the sky flickered. Just as it all went dark, thousands of screams went up. Thousands of endless screams. Time dragged on and on, and Jordan hoped for the scene to change, but the screams wouldn't end. They burned in his ears. Louder. More hateful.

Tears came up. Jordan began to hear his mother's scream above the rest. "MAMA!" he screamed back. "*MAMA!!*" But she didn't hear him. She just went on and on. In pain. Forever.

Jordan started beating the air, trying to reach her. His own screams blended in with the rest. He was trying to cut through the darkness when the pool spit him out. Jordan hit the stony ground, but it didn't hurt. Still, the screams kept echoing in his head. Even when there was complete silence now.

He was back. Safe and sound. Soaking wet, maybe, but unharmed. For a moment, he sat there, taking it all in. Then, he began to weep and sob. His mother. His helpless mother! Gone. No amount of sacrifice could save her. He was sure of it. She was lost in the shadows, like his father. And like his father and the rest of them, she had become a shadow herself. Finally and without end. In a place called *The End.* Where the screams would *never* end.

The thought of this made his breaths shorten and his crying even heavier. Would his own torment end? It was only a day ago when he was safe in his home with his mother by his side. Sure, she was dying, but she was there. And he was there. And they were together. But now he knew they would never be together. No matter where Jordan went or how long he'd be there for, his mother would always be screaming in that dark, cold place. This thought hurt him more than anything that came before. It made his stomach tie up in knots. Made him want to roll over and die.

Yes, he *would* die. But not just yet. It had to happen at the right moment. The way the prophecy said it. To be honest, Jordan didn't want to die. He realized that he didn't care about anyone else. Okay, it was a selfish thought, but it was true. The only one he wanted to save was his mother. Maybe his father, too. But that seemed impossible now. Who else was there that he wanted to save? Not those townspeople who seemed bent on hating him.

A wave of confusion came over Jordan. Answers? The Water King promised answers! Sure, there were *some* answers. But they came with even more questions. This made Jordan *really* angry. His lips pressed together tightly. His eyes became slanted. His eyebrows pushed closer together. His cheeks grew hotter.

He sat there for a good, long while. Eyeing the glowing waters but not really watching them. Eventually, he heard voices.

"Come back, come back," the waters whispered gently to him.

Jordan sat there another minute, not ready to move. He let a few more tears go, wiped his dripping nose with the back of his hand, and then stood up.

Once he put both feet into the stream, it quickly rushed him back to the large room with the upside down waterfall. Jordan climbed out of the waters and laid himself on a rock. He looked bitterly at the waterfall, his breathing heavy.

Where was the Water King? Jordan didn't want to come back to this place. Not now. But here he was. Waiting.

Some more time passed before the king appeared inside the circling waters. He stared at Jordan for a while, and Jordan stared back. Both of them didn't say anything for a bit. But the king ended up speaking first.

"You have been through so much," he said to the boy. Jordan didn't say anything. It was true. He knew it. There was no need to confirm. His worn-out face gave it away clearly. "I'm sure you want your answers now."

Another true statement. Where did Jordan want to start? The scenes flashed by so quickly. "I don't understand what happened," he said. This was general enough that Jordan hoped the king's explanation would cover many of his questions.

And it did. The Water King clarified to Jordan what he saw within the pool. Starting from the beginning…His parents knew the king. They grew up where both sides of the world were connected. The king took a special liking to Jordan's parents. "For no particular reason," the king made sure to add. But they were chosen, handpicked by the Water King, to lead the town he started.

The king's rivers flowed through the town. They provided a way to live, but something else, too. It gave life itself. Drinking it would not only heal them of any injury, but it would keep them from dying. Always. This meant that the waters that healed Jordan also had the ability to give him life that lasted forever.

When his father was appointed mayor by the Water King, he was told to make sure not to drink any other water source. To do so would break the deal they had made. All the town had to do was drink the king's waters — and only the king's waters — and everyone would be able to live without end. To do the opposite was unthinkable.

At one point, a meadow person came. Someone who did not like the Water King or his favored town. So it offered a different water source. Lied. Said it was the king's. It said this to trick his parents. To cut off the deal and separate the town from the king forever.

It worked. The moment the waters went down his father's throat, the deal was suddenly broken.

Suddenly, and without the ability to be changed back.

The Water King went on to tell Jordan that this broken deal was more than just a loss of water privileges. It brought on a curse. The special, life-giving waters were cut off from the well and hidden from the town.

"I had to do it," said the king. "Or the town would be gone for good. Lost to the poison forever. There would be no hope for them if they continued drinking my waters. It would only seal their doom."

One drop from those sparkling waters poisoned everything. It didn't just slowly kill all those who drank it, but it became their *everything*. People tried leaving, the king told Jordan. But the poison was so addictive. Everyone soon came back. It provided temporary relief, even though it killed them much quicker.

Jordan asked about the shadow man. Curious how it turned into a shadow, and how his parents didn't. "Its fate was already sealed," said the king.

"So were my parents'," Jordan said.

"Not quite," the king replied.

Jordan tilted his head. His eyes narrowed on the Water King. *Not quite? Then, how so?*

The king went on to tell Jordan about the prophecy. "There's still hope, Jo!"

"But I saw my parents…" Jordan broke off. Yes, he saw many people turn into shadows. And he definitely heard his mother's endless screams.

The Water King assured him that what he saw at the end was what would take place if the prophecy failed. If the poisoned waters weren't changed.

Jordan still didn't understand why it had to be this way. Why he had to die to make it pure.

This was where the king paused. He took in Jordan's sad and hopeless face.

"So brave," said the king. "But *you* cannot do it."

This made Jordan look up. Cannot do it? Can't do what? *Die*? Save his mother? But he was the pure one. The only one who was kept safe from the poison all these years. Yes, he *had* to be the one. The prophecy said so. Otherwise, it *would* fail.

But Jordan was told something he never

thought about. The king told him that he, Jordan, was one of them. Tainted. Poisoned. *Trapped.*

"It's in your blood," said the king, "the moment you were conceived."

It made sense. Jordan's parents had the poison in themselves. In their blood. No amount of outside protection could keep the poison from spreading on the inside. From it being passed onto their children. Onto Jordan.

"Your parents thought they could save you," said the king. "But they didn't know."

So all those years tucked away in the woods did nothing. All those times staying home while his mother went to town, meaningless. All that effort making sure he met no one. All those basins of rainwater. All that hope that one day he could leave. It was all for nothing. Nothing…

This news might have been the worst news of all. It made his breathing stop. His eyes droop. His mind go blank. All Jordan could do now was feel the full weight of helplessness settle on him. It pulled him down into hopelessness.

"So the prophecy," Jordan said quietly, "isn't true. I can't save them."

"No," said the king.

Those words stuck with Jordan during the silence. It felt like a really long time.

The king added, "But it wasn't talking about you."

PART VII
THE WELL

It was the Water King. *He* was the one who the prophecy was speaking about. Jordan was just the messenger. The forerunner. "The *catalyst*," the king told him. This was a new word for Jordan. He mouthed it to himself as the king kept explaining.

Apparently, there was even more to the prophecy than Jordan had already been told. The Water King spoke kindly when he asked the waters to sing it to Jordan one last time. This time, all the way through. So, they did.

The boy is here; The boy, at last
The boy through evil wood had passed
And now is here to tell the king

That he would end the water's sting

He would by flesh to them return
To then confront the dark cistern
By blood so pure a drop would do
And make the dirty waters new

Death can only keep the ill and
Must spit up who are not poisoned
For life so bright cannot decay
This the boy will surely survey

So Jordan would watch whatever it was that was meant to happen. This was his purpose. This was the plan. To see the *Water King* die. *Not* to be the one to do it himself. It was a bit of a relief, Jordan came to think of it. He could feel his body relax. But he didn't say this to the king. Was he really supposed to be happy that another person was taking his place?

There was still concern on the boy's face. The Water King noticed this. It was about his mother. Jordan still couldn't get her screams out of his head.

"She's not gone yet," the king said tenderly. He went on to tell Jordan that the next step was to purify the poisoned waters. The only way to reverse the curse. "At the well," it was added. "Only then will your mother be able to drink from the living waters. And that includes you, Jo."

That's right. He needed the purified waters just as much as his mother. They needed to drink it to undo the poisoning. To clean out their systems. So death would spit them back up. That's what the prophecy said. And that's what the Water King affirmed.

"But we need to go now," the Water King said. "There's no time to lose."

Jordan got to his feet, and that's when he realized something very important. The Water King wasn't made of flesh at all. He was made of water. He had no blood in him.

But this didn't seem to throw off the king. Jordan was told to step back from the rising waterfall. So he did.

The king, who had been inside that waterfall this whole time — maybe forever — stretched out his hand. Skin appeared as his arm went through the watery curtain. His face came out next, but the watery crown disappeared. Jordan thought maybe a real, golden one would replace it. But only a headful of hair was showing. The king fell on the flat, stony ground. Completely naked. Bent over. Weak. Yes, the Water King was all skin now, which meant there must be blood in him, too. Blood to give.

Jordan stood there for a minute. He had been told to back up, so he didn't want to make a bad move. But when the king himself made no stir, he thought it was time to do a check-up.

He was afraid. Jordan didn't want to make the king upset by getting too close. But he had to do something. The boy's body shook a little as he went up to the king, now a helpless, naked man. He called to the king, not sure what else to do.

This was very strange to Jordan. It wasn't so much that he saw a watery figure turn into a human being. It was that Jordan had once seen a big, powerful king stand up straight. Now, he was trying to lend a hand to that same person who was now like jelly on the floor.

The king's hand rose up, trying to find the boy.

Jordan took it, understanding that he wanted help. It took all of Jordan's strength to bring the wobbly king to his knees and then to his feet.

The king's voice sounded tired at first. But as he kept speaking, it seemed to return to a more normal state. He leaned on Jordan as he guided him toward the exit and out of the cave.

There was a small gathering of meadow people outside the entrance. They all bowed low as Jordan and the king stepped out into the bright outdoors. It took a moment for the boy to realize that what the people were doing didn't have to do with *him*. It was the Water King they were paying tribute to. It was interesting to him that they recognized their ruler. Now a human. And without clothes.

Just as Jordan thought of it, a meadow person came to the front. It held a folded stack of what looked like sowed-together leaves. Of course, it was leaves.

The king touched the meadow person. It was a kind touch. A way to say *thank you* before taking the bundle of leaves. He unraveled it, and Jordan could tell it was the meadow people's attempt at making clothes. It was one long shirt. Like a dress, really. A summer dress. Jordan couldn't help but grin a little, thinking of his mother, who often wore a similar warm-colored dress. And how he and her would dance around their house. Sometimes to music. Sometimes just to each other's laughs.

Jordan turned serious once he noticed the king was eyeing him. But the king didn't look offended at all. Still, Jordan guessed the king knew why he was smiling.

Some people from the gathering helped the king put it on. Yes, it was a dress. And it didn't look that comfortable. But the king seemed very happy at his gift. He would definitely be cold once they went back to the other side. Well, at least he wasn't naked anymore.

Then, something odd happened. The meadow people started crying. *Crying.* Jordan had never seen an emotion like that come out of a meadow person before. But the king explained that they knew what he was about to do. Jordan told him how they hadn't seemed to understand his own pain. But the king told him their memories of humans were wiped clean when the curse happened.

"Just for a time," the Water King added. "Until both lands are connected once again."

So, Jordan's world and the Water King's world would be joined back together one day? He liked that idea. Still, this didn't help him understand why the meadow people were emotional around the king and not him.

"They never knew what it was like to be without me," the king told Jordan. "Until now."

Jordan imagined the meadow people and the waters and all the other creatures he didn't know about. He imagined them being really close to the king. It reminded him how he would feel sad and lonely when his mother went into town alone. Even just for a few hours. He had always wanted to go with her. But she insisted on traveling alone. Jordan had understood. But it didn't make it any easier.

The king kept leaning on Jordan as they made their way down the watery slope and past the large lake and vast meadow. The two were about to enter the woods when Jordan stopped. Scared. The king promised him that the shadow man wouldn't be waiting for them.

"He's at the square this very minute," he said.

That's where they needed to get to. But the king asked that the two stop off at his house beforehand. Jordan didn't know why at first. But then, he looked at how unprepared the king was. A thin, leafy dress with no sleeves. And no shoes, either. It was about to get cold quick. He needed proper clothing.

The king took a deep breath as they officially stepped into the woods. The two went down a little hill, and that's when Jordan felt the cold coming on. The water was still warm, thankfully. But the trees, once so green, began to look quite dead. Eventually, there were no leaves on any of them.

A lot of time must have passed. The woods used to be colored with bright reds and yellows and oranges. That was when Jordan took his mother to get help. Now, no leaf remained. Yes, a lot of time was now gone...

The king seemed to know where to go. He now led Jordan through the woods. It was a long walk, but the king finally got his footing. Jordan didn't have to be his support after a short while.

There it was. Jordan's home. The home that was his safe place all these years. The home that brought light and warmth because of his mother. The home that saw their happy times. The home that saw their sad times. And especially those last moments…

Jordan turned to look at the king walking ahead of him toward the front door. Maybe Jordan's house wasn't the only one who saw all this. All their joys and pain. And this comforted him a little.

They walked inside. Jordan's first glance was to the left. His mother's room. That bed, now empty. There was a chill in the air. Like some type of cold wind coming from that place. Jordan decided to avoid it.

The king walked around in the kitchen. He looked in cabinets but found nothing. Nothing that he was looking for, Jordan knew. It was food they needed. Both of them were feeling it. But that hope was gone now. The last can of soup went to his mother.

The king told Jordan that he was thirsty. That,

at least, Jordan could fix. He went over to the large basin near the window. A rush of cold wind came in as he slid it open. He dunked two empty glasses into it, then gave one to the king. Both of them tried drinking it. It felt colder than ice going down.

The next stop was his father's room. This was the room his mother used to sleep in. But when she got sick, she decided to go to the one closest to the kitchen. She said she did this so she could make sure Jordan was doing his homework at the table. But really, it was so she could be closer to him. And Jordan liked that.

Jordan turned on the closet light. He hadn't been in here before. His mother never wanted him to. So he never did. But now, the king needed clothes. He was pretty sure his mother would understand.

Jordan's fingers touched the different fabrics. Some soft. Soft a bit rough. But all of them cold because the drafty house. He tried connecting them to memories, but he realized he didn't really have any memories of his father. This made him sad.

Jordan left the king to change. The door closed as he went back into the short hallway. He thought about stoking a fire but realized they would have to leave for town soon. So he put his hands in his pockets instead.

Jordan stood outside near the meadow. He watched the tips of the grass flow like waves on the sea. This was where his mother and father chased each other. Maybe where they fell in love. He tried imagining them in the field. Tried hard to think of them running his way, chasing *him*. With happy faces and excited laughs.

That thought soon passed. It was hard to keep when he knew what was really true. Both of them were lost in this place called The End. And poor Jordan was here. At least the king was with him.

When Jordan returned to check up on the king, he found him sitting on a chest at the end of his father's bed. He was putting boots on. Jordan took him in. That red woolen sweater. Those brown-looking jeans. Charcoal boots.

Jordan and the king watched each other for a moment. The king's content face felt inviting. So Jordan went closer. In just a few steps, he and the king were only a foot or two apart. Their eyes were almost level with each other.

Was this what a father looked like? With a dark, curly beard and big brown eyes? With eyes so warm? The king's were the warmest he had ever seen.

Jordan reached out a hand. Placed it on the king's cheek. The king didn't move. He let Jordan feel his face. Touch his scratchy beard. Jordan liked that. A sudden joy lit inside. It made him smile. The king smiled back.

The two watched each other for another minute or two. Then, Jordan slowly went into the king's arms and laid his head on his shoulder. He was simply curious. The boy wanted to feel what it was like to be held by a father. Arms were soon wrapped around him. One of the king's big hands held Jordan firmly by the waist. The other softly waved through his hair like a comb. The king was warm. Tender, like his mother. But so strong that all of Jordan's fears were wiped away when he was in those arms.

He could have stayed there for a long time. Listening to the king's heart beating slowly. *Buh-*

bum...Buh-bum... But after a few minutes, the king's arms let Jordan go. His big, firm hands were placed on his shoulders now. And the king told him that it was time to go. That the prophecy needed to be fulfilled.

That's right. The prophecy. Jordan totally forgot. Being in his home with the king *felt* like home. He sighed, knowing in his heart that this couldn't last forever. So he nodded.

They put on hats and gloves and extra coats to keep themselves warm. Jordan took one final look at his mother's bed as they went out the door for the last time.

The king let Jordan hold his hand as they followed the path toward the road. Jordan didn't want to let go. It was like having a father. *Finally*. Even if it *was* only for a little bit longer.

Jordan tried having some conversation with the king. He wanted to know what it was like being a king. What it was like to live on the other side. How it felt to turn into a man. Why he let the town get poisoned just to get himself killed for it. But the king was strangely quiet. When Jordan looked up to see his face, there was fear in the king's eyes. Fear and sadness. He could feel the king's hand shake as he held it. In the end, the two walked in silence. Jordan gripped the king's hand tightly. The king gripped back.

There was the sign now. *Brookfield.* That poisoned town. Jordan noticed tears coming down from the king's eyes when they passed it. Was he crying because of the town and how the people were trapped in it? Or was it because he was about to die? Jordan never asked.

Before the two even saw any buildings, they could hear it. A faint noise. Like a festival was going on somewhere. Jordan was right. When the two went around the bend and saw the square straight ahead, he noticed the well was completely hidden by a sea of townspeople. The king led Jordan along the forest's edge and to the back of one of the three-story buildings facing the square. There was a ladder that made its way to the top.

"This is where I leave you," said the king. His voice proved that he was struggling to keep it together.

Jordan touched the king's face again. This time, it was to wipe the tear stains from his cheeks. This made the king smile, even through all that pain he must have felt. It was a weak smile, but it was still warm.

The boy asked him a question. He couldn't help it. "Why are you so scared?" he asked.

The king didn't need time to think about it. "Because I've never been apart from my father. Not until right now."

His father? The Water King had a *father*? So, was this king just a prince? How could there be two kings? But, after all, he was speaking to a man who was once a different form. Who didn't always have a beard and skin. Who was once water through and through. Why couldn't there be two kings?

"Why do *you* have to do it?" Jordan asked.

Because, really, there must have been people out there who weren't tainted by the water. Where they didn't have the poison in their blood. On the other side, maybe.

This time, the king hesitated. His eyes grew heavy. It drooped a little. "There's no other way." And the king told Jordan that no person had the ability to reverse the poisoned waters. No one on this side *or* the other side. Not even if a thousand of them shed their blood. Hearing this made Jordan realize that the king was precious. Maybe that was why a single drop of *his* blood would do.

Jordan had a hundred more questions, but they heard people coming. Just on the other side of the building. Coming down the alley. The king urged Jordan to climb up to the roof and stay hidden. Jordan wanted to ask what he was supposed to do after all this happened, but there was no time. So Jordan climbed the tall ladder and hid himself on the flat roof of the building. Right when he did this, a group of men appeared around the wall.

"Don't recognize this one," said one of them in a raspy voice.

They made mocking jokes at the king. Jokes not worth repeating. Then, one of them hit him with their fist. It looked like they used all their force. The king tumbled over, now red in the face. Why wasn't he *doing* anything? Jordan could barely watch. But this was the king's purpose. To die. And Jordan's was to watch it happen. It was hard to do.

The men laughed at the king before picking

him up by the collar. He was still awake, but he seemed dizzy. Out of it. They dragged him through the alley. Jordan crawled along the roof to the other side, surveying the square and the well in the middle. But he saw much more than that. Jordan couldn't find the stony street because it was covered by townspeople. Little fires were going on in different areas. A bit of chaos here and there.

The crowd opened up like a seam. Making way for the king and the men carrying him. There were chants and laughs that sounded very mean. The men tied the king's hands behind his back and threw him on the ground next to the well. Jordan saw that the king wasn't the only one. There were six others. All of them looked scared. The king was still recovering from the smack in the face.

People in the crowd took turns doing whatever they wanted to that group of seven helpless people. Spit. Punch. Kick. Pretty soon, most of them were lying on the ground with red all over them. The king was one of them.

Then, in the corner of Jordan's eye, he saw something that made him stoop even lower. A shadow with green slits for eyes made its way through the crowd. *The shadow man*. This scene reminded Jordan of one of the memories he saw in the upside-down pool. That scene where the shadow man forced innocent people to drink the water. Was this something they did every year? Did they kidnap people from other towns and force them here just for fun? Did those prisoners know what was about to happen? A frozen chill crawled up Jordan's body.

The shadow man walked around the tied-up people. Taking in the sight with great joy. But once it caught sight of the king's face, its own fell. Was the shadow man not expecting the king? How did it know what the king looked like? Well, it made sense, Jordan thought. The meadow people were able to recognize the king in his human form. And the shadow man *was* one of them at one point.

Surprised. That's a good word. The shadow man looked *very* surprised. Then, a mixture of fear and anger appeared. Jordan thought the shadow man would be jumping for joy at seeing the king. Knowing it had him. But it was quite the opposite. It looked as if the shadow man knew why the king was here. And it wasn't happy about it.

Still, the shadow man didn't let the king go. Instead, this only made the shadow man's madness grow. "Strip them!" it ordered.

Then, every single one of them were stood up on their feet. Their hats and coats were forced from them. Then, their shirts, pants, shoes, and the rest. All seven of them were completely bare. Just as the king entered humanity, so he was going to leave. Naked. Weak.

The shadow man commanded that large buckets of water be poured on them. Jordan remembered how the boys dripped poisoned water on him.

He watched the water be poured over the king. Then, something he didn't expect happened. All seven of them let out terrible screams. This made Jordan think of all those endless, helpless shrieks. *His mother…* Was this what those shadowy people were experiencing? Were they in an endless, dark sea of stinging waters? Was that their punishment?

Well, this was the *king's* punishment. A punishment he didn't deserve. His body was burned red. All of the prisoners were that way. But the shadow man had a second and a third bucket dumped on the king alone. The king fell over and wouldn't get up. This made the shadow man happy again.

Jordan noticed a fight taking place in the crowd. Right in front of the king. It looked as if they were each wanting to hurt him. Instead, they began pulling each other. Seeing who would win out. At one point, one of the two was sliced in the face with the other's knife.

Jordan watched as that wounded man fell. His face was next to the king's. And then, another thing he didn't expect happened. He saw the king staring at the hurt man right beside him. He stretched out his hand. It looked difficult to do with all the pain he was in. But still, he stretched it out. And the king placed his hand on the wounded man's face. Before Jordan could really take in the moment, the man's face was completely healed. This didn't make the man look grateful. It made him look very afraid, actually. Afraid of the king. Soon, that man ran away and was lost in the crowd.

The man that won the fight got his prize. He poured more water on the king. This time, with slow dribbles. Like the boys who had hurt Jordan in the woods.

The shadow man eventually shooed the man away. It wanted to get on with the evening. All seven of the naked, burned prisoners were driven in a line. The shadow man directed some townspeople to force the waters down people's throats. Some resisted, but none of them were able to stop them. Once it went down their throats, they began choking. Like Jordan's mother and father.

But when it came to the king, it was the shadow man who faced him. It became a stare-down. Those green eyes against those deep brown ones. The shadow man pinched the king's jaws, trying to force his mouth open. For the first time, the king resisted. The shadow man tried harder. It wouldn't open. Then, the shadow man had men try to open the king's mouth for him. This also didn't work. Somehow, the king was able to keep his mouth shut.

This made the shadow man *very* angry. Without

thought, the shadow man waved its arm. A large, red line was slashed over the king's stomach. The redness grew and grew. "Dunk him," said the shadow man.

Many men closed in on the king and tied a thick rope around him. A rope that was tied to the top of the well. Then, many other men tugged on the rope. The king was forced into the air, right above the well. Jordan saw the king look his way. It was that look that he knew meant *goodbye.* Jordan couldn't help but feel a sharp pain. Right where his heart was.

Then, the men let go of the rope, and the king quickly disappeared into the well. Gone.

PART VIII
THE END

The king wasn't dead. He couldn't be. Jordan wouldn't let the thought in. Not at first. But when the shadow man let out a terrible laugh, he realized it was over. The Water King *was* dead.

Jordan knew it. He knew this was going to happen. But unlike those townspeople, Jordan knew what it meant. He grew sick in his stomach as he watched the crowd parade around the well. Round and round. Chanting. Laughing. Having a *good time*. This was far from how Jordan felt about all this. He wasn't expecting it, but it was about the worst pain he ever felt. Maybe even worse than losing his mother. Sure, he didn't know the king for very long. But he felt as if he had come to know him well enough. After seeing all the king had left behind just to die in a poisoned well, Jordan felt for him. He also missed his strong hugs. His firm hands. He missed the king looking at him with those warm eyes.

Jordan cupped his ears with his hands. He wanted the townspeople to stop. The noise only made it more painful. But it went on and on for hours. Jordan lay down on the flat roof and tried focusing on the crystal clear sky. That big, bright moon. All those little stars. It was impossible.

He was able to sleep eventually. When he woke up, he saw that the sky was slightly brighter. It wasn't black anymore. There was a hint of blue now. And the moon was almost under the tree line.

Jordan listened. It was quiet. He slowly turned over to his stomach and crawled along the rooftop. The square was completely empty. Nothing but the icy wind running through it. Come to think of it, Jordan was *freezing*.

He saw that there were red spots all over the stony pavement. A reminder that last night did actually happen. He wondered if anyone would ever clean that up.

Jordan's eyes focused on the well. The king's body still had to be there. Lifeless. There was a sharp pang of anger. He didn't want the king to be left in that place. Did people have no heart?

He was going to do it. He would try to get the king's body back up somehow. Jordan didn't know how he would do that or even how he would get in there safely. But this was what he was going to do. The prophecy didn't bind him to sit by watch anymore. In fact, Jordan didn't know exactly *what* was going to happen next.

The first thing to do was to get off that roof. So Jordan slipped down the ladder and hid himself in the alleyway. He glanced around the square one last time. No one.

He ran quietly to the well and looked in. It was too dark in there. He couldn't make out anything. And the rope was gone. The men from the crowd must have thrown it in with the king.

The fires weren't burning anymore. But Jordan went over to find hot coals still glowing. He could make a fire if he wanted to. His mother taught him years ago. So he could learn how to light the fireplace. Jordan realized now that she was preparing him for his survival. When she would be gone, leaving him all by himself.

Making a fire out here in the open was dangerous. Jordan knew that. But what other choice did he have? He was determined to find the king's body.

Jordan went looking for some small twigs and larger branches. He even found a nice, thick piece that could be used as a torch. It took about ten minutes of trying before the fire caught. When it finally did start, Jordan realized he needed oil or something for the torch. There were a few rusty barrels near the back that had a skull and bones on it. Jordan had seen that in a textbook before. It was worth a shot.

He went over to the barrels. Thankfully, the sky was getting a bit bright now. He could read what was on there. *Kerosene*. Jordan never heard of that word. He wasn't sure if it would work, but he tried it anyway. He took off his coat and outer layers to get to his white undershirt. After he put the rest of his clothes back on, he wrapped his white shirt over the giant branch and knotted it. Then, he dunked the shirt into the kerosene.

Quickly. He had to do this quickly. Jordan ran back to the fire. Without any pause, the shirt lit up. The oil-like liquid must have worked. Back at the well, Jordan used the torch to see if he could see anything. It was faint. Maybe it was the bottom of the well. He wasn't sure.

Jordan decided to drop the torch to see what might happen. Like he thought, it splashed into the water, and the light disappeared. But this helped Jordan figure out how far down it was. Not that far. Just like jumping off a tall diving board. The ones he would see in books. Of course, he never had the chance to jump off one himself.

Yes, Jordan was going to do it. He didn't know what might happen next, but it seemed like a better place in there than being exposed out in the open. Where he could get tortured. Just like the king.

Jordan wondered about the waters for a second. Should he even jump in there if it was going to hurt him? The waters hurt the innocent people. It burned the king very badly. But it never hurt *him* when the boys poured the poison on him. It never stung. Was it because it was already in his bloodstream?

Still, the king came to *end the waters' sting*. That's what the prophecy foretold. Either way, the waters shouldn't be able to hurt Jordan. And also, what else was there to lose? His mother and father were gone. The king was dead. He might as well take his chances. So he jumped.

Jordan couldn't feel the bottom of it. This was a *big* well. Like a pool, but dark. And something else, too. *Warm*. The waters were warm! What the king did must have worked!

Jordan was thankful he could swim. Or else, he would likely drown. Come to think of it, the Water King was probably at the bottom of the well. Far under the water. There was no way he could get the body back. He saw that now. It was hopeless.

Just as sadness rose up in his chest, Jordan saw those green slits for eyes. Did the shadow man follow him in there? Or did it know to hide? To wait for him in this place?

Jordan took in a deep breath and prepared himself for the pain. The coldness. The screams...

But they never came. In fact, when he looked a little closer, the shadow man didn't seem to be staring at him at all. Its eyes were glossed over.

Jordan wished he could see what was around him. It was very dark except for the hole at the top that showed the early morning sky.

But he didn't need to wish for too long. The waters began to glow. Like the healing waters on the other side. Pretty soon, the whole underground area could be seen. Jordan noticed that the shadow man was shaking. As if the waters were cold. It didn't seem big and mighty anymore. It looked helpless. If it had teeth, it would be chattering.

Jordan saw something else, too. The king's body. It *was* down there at the bottom. He was tempted to look away because he didn't want to remember the king like that. He wanted to think of the king's warm eyes looking back at him.

But there was a glow that grew brighter and brighter. Like a current within the waters. A swirling branch of light soon reached the king's body, and that's when it happened. The entire waters turned white. They were so bright they blinded Jordan. They did more than that, too.

The next thing he knew, he was lying on a ledge. Jordan was still deep in the well. The water was still glowing, even if it wasn't as bright anymore. And he was still wet. It didn't seem like much time passed.

Then, there he was. The king, sitting on the ledge next to Jordan, playing with his hair. *Alive!* Jordan turned to sit up. The eyes — so very warm! Looking back at him! Jordan rushed into the king's arms. Strong. Secure. And he stayed there for a long time. He wouldn't let go. Not this time.

The king wasn't naked anymore. He was wearing some sort of human clothes. Jordan wasn't sure how he got them. They weren't his father's.

He was still human. *Fully* human. But his skin was no longer covered in burns. He assumed the slice in the stomach was gone, too.

The king gently pulled Jordan away so they could look at each other. His big hands with those strong fingers felt the boy's face. Like how Jordan had done to him. It was a tender touch. First, his cheek. Then, a quick one on the lips. And then, the king said, "drink."

He was referring to the waters. Jordan got back into the pool without question. He was a bit nervous, he had to admit. These waters used to kill. But he trusted the king. So Jordan slowly went deeper under the water until his mouth was fully submerged.

Sweet. Very sweet. And *warm.* It didn't smell like wormwood anymore. Not even like sweet peas. Something different. Something new.

Jordan felt it. It happened inside him. It was hard for him to explain the feeling. But it was like he was being fixed on. His growing hunger went away. His thirst disappeared. His aches were gone. The king had done it. He ended the sting!

Jordan looked over at the shadow man, who was still shaking in the water. He asked the king what happened to it. "Something beyond my help," he replied.

"So it's dying," Jordan said.

"*Defeated*, yes. *Dying*, not quite. Not yet, at least. It still has some time left."

Jordan looked over with great worry. The king told the boy how the shadow man would soon grow very angry. Angry toward those who would drink the water. Make war against the town. Apparently, this wasn't the end.

"But the war's already been won," said the king confidently. "And it won't last forever. I promise."

And the king told Jordan that one day, the shadow man will be locked up in that horrifying place called *The End*. "And it will never escape," he said with finality to it.

Jordan wanted to ask why this had to happen. Why the king didn't just finish it off right then. Finish the war once and for all. The king took some time to reply. "There are people out there who still need my water," he said.

This had to happen before the king could end it. Jordan understood. His mother still had the poison in her. Still lost in that dark, shadowy place with the rest of them. He didn't want the king to end it all before she drank the water. Yes, the king's patience was a kindness.

"Go," said the king. "Take these waters. Find your mother."

The king took a flask out of his pocket. It wasn't made of clay, like the one Jordan had been given by the meadow people. And it wasn't glass like the shadow man gave to his parents. It was smooth and made of metal. And it held a lot more water than the others.

Jordan placed it under the water and capped it. And before he could ask the king any questions, the waters began to swirl like a funnel. Soon, he was trapped by its force. He was being pulled down. Down, down, down. Soon, the king was lost by the glowing, rushing water all around him. The warmth went cold, and Jordan found himself on land. A cold, wintery place. A place that looked a bit red from the dim sky. *The End.*

All Jordan could make out were a few snow-covered hills. Hills and bodies. It was hard to see because the falling snow was thick here. And the wind was biting. But, at least Jordan was still under his many layers of clothes. And somehow, it was all suddenly dry now. This helped.

The next thing he saw helped even more. The king was standing beside him. It was strange. The king was not dressed for the weather, but he seemed all right. He didn't even have any shoes on.

The king stretched out his hand. Jordan took it. It kept him warm. The two walked on. For miles and miles, they passed iced-over bodies. Sort of like statues. At one point, Jordan had to pause. The faces of these ones were familiar. *The boys*. The ones who attacked him in the woods. The ones who stole his medicine. The ones who tried killing him. They were now here. Now dead and gone. Their eyes looked *very* cold. Was his mother this way, too?

It was odd that the king kept on moving. That he didn't seem to want to stop. When Jordan looked up, he found that the king was gone. Nowhere to be seen. Jordan called out to the king, but there was no response. Jordan tried following the king's footprints but became lost in the sea of bodies and newly fallen snow.

Some more time passed before Jordan found people who were somehow alive. He could tell they were because their bodies were shaking.

"Help!" Jordan heard. He quickly looked over to see a woman scrunched up on the ground. Like the rest of them. But she held out her hand. "*Please!*"

Help? How? Well, Jordan sort of knew. He was holding it in his hands. But this woman wasn't his mother. The king didn't tell him to help anyone else. And honestly, he didn't want to. He had to get to his mother as soon as possible. But the mixed pain in this woman's voice was hard to ignore. She did need help. That wasn't hard to tell.

Jordan poured just a tiny bit of water into the cap before handing it to her. She drank it down quickly. In a single moment, her frozen body stopped shaking and began to move freely. The color of her skin turned back to normal. As if the ice inside her was melting.

The woman grabbed his arm. Jordan was scared that she would steal the entire flask for herself. But she brought him in and hugged him. It was a warm hug.

Jordan didn't know what the woman should do next. So he told her to wait until he found the king. The king would know what to do. As he went on, one eye on finding the king, the other on finding his mother, another person cried out for help. This time, it was an old man.

Jordan hesitated. But another cap was filled and brought to the man's mouth. The old man's body became as warm as the woman before him. On he went, but more and more people called out to Jordan for help. *"Help! Help! Help!"* It sounded like an endless line of people were trying to get a taste of the waters. Apparently, they knew what Jordan was trying to keep to himself. But he only had so much and worried he wouldn't have enough for his mother.

Not everyone around asked for help. Some actually wanted Jordan to get far away from them. Even to the point of calling him horrible names. But to those who asked for help, Jordan did the best he could. This took a long time. To his surprise, the flask never ran out. But he could feel it getting down to the bottom. There wasn't much left now.

With every person who called out to him, he hoped he saw his mother's face. Or, at least, be able to find the king. It felt more and more hopeless as time went on. As the waters were almost completely gone. Why hadn't the king given him more flasks? Or a bucket?

Jordan was about to turn around to go back to where he came from. To try to find the king. That's when he heard it. It was his mother's voice.

But she didn't cry out for help. She called out his name.

"Jo," she said. Jordan knew that voice. It was gentle. And kind. But weak. Very weak.

Jordan turned around to see his mother. She was so thin. Her lips were glossy because of the ice on them. He didn't understand how some people didn't died here in these conditions. Jordan's mother must have been in this place for weeks. Maybe even a month or two.

"Mama!" He fell on his knees. The snow was fighting to bury her, so he quickly made a trench around. His heart was beating so fast as he tried to warm her up with his body. Of course, this wouldn't work. Not here at the end of the world.

He tried moving her up to a sitting position. It was no use. She was stuck to the ground. But it didn't matter. He could still get the flask to her mouth. Jordan's hands shook so hard as he tried to get the flask out of his coat pocket. But he felt it leave his hand just as he opened the cap. His mother had knocked it away.

Jordan scrambled to get it back. The little that was left inside made its way onto the snow. His heart sank.

He quickly topped the flask. Yes, he could hear it. There was a tiny bit left. Ever so slight. Maybe just a few drops. Hopefully, this was enough. It had to be. Jordan had no other options left.

"Please, Mama!" Jordan told her. "This will heal you!"

But his mother held out an arm to stop him from putting it near her. Her face looked upset. She clearly didn't want it. *"Please!"* he begged. But she wouldn't have it. Not even a drop. Not for him. Not even for herself.

This was it. All of Jordan's efforts felt wasted now. His journey into town to get the medicine. Trying to give her the healing stream. The strength he used to help her through the woods. His time with the Water King. All of it. Everything. It was all for nothing. She was going to die. Be left in this terrible place. Not because she wasn't allowed to live. But for some reason, she didn't want to. Or, at least, she didn't want the *only thing* that could make her live.

"Please, Mama!" Jordan whined. Tears began pouring down his face as he placed his hand on her frozen cheeks. It was an ugly cry. Heavy. Deep. A sadness rose up. It felt more powerful than anything he felt before. A hopelessness that tugged harder on him now more than ever.

He was leaning over his mother, still in tears, when he heard someone coming his way. Jordan looked up. It was the Water King. Finally, he was here.

"She doesn't want it!" Jordan said quickly. The king didn't seem confused or troubled. The calm look on his face upset Jordan more. "Help her!" he demanded. Jordan had never demanded anything before. He always went along. Always did what he was told — for the most part. "You promised!" His shouts turned to whines.

Jordan cried it out for a while. The king bent down and placed his hand on Jordan's shoulder. He gave the boy that look he had shown before. One of comfort. Then, Jordan said in a steady voice, "Do you even want to?"

Jordan thought the king's answer might simply be *yes*. But he said, "Not everyone will escape this place." The boy assumed that meant *no*.

But it wasn't a *no*. After the king said what he

said, he kindly pushed Jordan to the side. His mother looked at the king, who looked down at her. There was compassion in his eyes. He placed his thumb over her lips like he did with Jordan. Then, he told Jordan to give his mother the water.

The boy was afraid that, in her anger, she would spill the final drops on the ground. But she wasn't angry anymore. By the looks of it, it seemed to Jordan that she was waiting for it now. Wanting it. What did the Water King do?

"Is that why some people wanted the water and others didn't?" Jordan asked the king. "Because you touched some and not others?" The king's kind smile answered that question. Jordan was sure this meant *yes*.

Jordan poured the last few drops into the cap and tried handing it to the king. But the king told Jordan to do it. So he did. Jordan bent over, put the cap to his mother's lips, and carefully tilted it. In one drawn-out moment, her icy cold body felt gradually warmer. Her skin no longer looked colorless. She could move now. The first thing she did was reach out her arms. Jordan knew what that meant. It meant she was alive. She was healed.

Saved. He bent down and hugged her. The tightest hug he ever gave.

Yes, she was better now. Those eyes were warm. And so were her hands. *Very* warm. And even though she was shaking because of the wind, Jordan knew she would be okay. The king was right beside them, watching them. Smiling. Laughing. Jordan's mother saw this and pulled the king in by his shirt. Then, they were all huddled together. Warm and safe. And happy.

A thought grew in Jordan's mind. *His father*. He was here. Somewhere. Was he dead? Was he alive? Well, he'd been gone for seven years. He must be dead. But the king told Jordan that his father was still around. And when Jordan picked up the flask to find it somehow full again, it gave him a hopeful feeling. A warm feeling. He liked that.

* * *

Dear reader,

I am incredibly grateful that you have taken the time to journey through these pages. This story has been on my heart for a while, and I'm glad it's finally able to rest in your hands.

If this story has affected you in some positive way, would you be willing to leave a rating or review on Amazon or Goodreads? Doing so will help others feel confident to pick up this story, and it will help spread a message we all desperately need to hear.

Just like Jordan was sent on mission with a flask of healing waters, I would like to ask you if you'd be willing spread the word about this little book. Sharing it with friends, families, loved ones, coworkers, classrooms, book clubs, and other social groups means a world of difference.

THANK YOU!

Yours,
A.T. Lischak

P.S. Feel free to start a conversation with me on my website or through email. I'd love to hear from you!

author@atlischak.com
WWW.ATLISCHAK.COM

DISCUSSION GUIDE

INITIAL REFLECTION QUESTIONS

1. What scene resonated most with you? Why do you think it impacted you?
2. How did Jordan's character change throughout the story? What were some key turning points in his emotional growth?
3. What role does love play in this narrative? How does Jordan's relationship with his mother shape his decisions?
4. The story explores isolation and connection. How does Jordan's journey

from isolation to interacting with others reflect these themes?

5. What did you find most surprising about the Water King? Did your perception of him change throughout the narrative?
6. The shadow man represents deception and temptation. What are examples of his subtle manipulations? How did Jordan resist or fall prey to them?

THEMATIC EXPLORATION

1. What does the story teach about sacrifice? How do different characters (Jordan, the Water King) embody the idea of sacrifice? What do you think motivates Jordan to continue making sacrifices despite the dangers?
2. Discuss the theme of trust in the story. Who does Jordan trust, and who does he distrust? How does this affect his journey? Have there been times in your own life where trust or mistrust shaped an important decision?

3. What role does forgiveness play in the narrative? How does Jordan wrestle with forgiving his father? Why is forgiveness difficult, and how is it ultimately portrayed in the story?
4. How does the story depict hope in the face of despair? What moments reflect Jordan's persistence even when he feels hopeless? How do the healing waters symbolize hope or redemption?

MORAL DILEMMAS AND CHOICES

1. If you were in Jordan's position, would you have followed the shadow man's conditions? Why or why not?
2. What would you have done differently in Jordan's place? Were there moments where you disagreed with his actions?
3. Jordan was given a chance to leave his mother and escape the town's curse. Do you think he made the right decision to stay?

4. Do you think the Water King's sacrifice was inevitable? What other paths could the story have taken?

SYMBOLISM AND INTERPRETATION

1. The poisoned water plays a significant role in the narrative. How does it symbolize corruption, temptation, or human weakness?
2. Not every aspect of this story has an exact correlation to biblical ideas or truths. Are you able to point out parts of the book in which the author took liberties to make it original to the story?
3. Discuss the significance of the well and the healing waters. How do these elements represent transformation or redemption?
4. How does the story explore time and alternate realities? How does Jordan's experience in different realms reflect emotional and spiritual growth?

FAITH AND FAMILY

1. How does Jordan's journey reflect the struggle to have faith in God during difficult times? In what ways does his persistence, despite uncertainty and fear, mirror the challenges believers face when trusting God through trials?
2. What parallels can you draw between the Water King's sacrifice and the sacrifice of Christ? How does the story reflect the themes of atonement, redemption, and selfless love?
3. The story portrays moments of testing and temptation. How do these moments reflect spiritual trials believers face in their walk of faith? How can we apply Jordan's responses to our own experiences?
4. Jordan's unwavering loyalty to his mother is a central theme in the story. How does hid dedication reflect the biblical call to honor and care for parents? What can we learn from Jordan's sacrifice and

determination in loving his mother, even when it was difficult and painful?

APPLICATIONS TO PERSONAL LIFE

1. How can the themes of redemption and sacrifice apply to your life?
2. Have you ever been in a situation where you needed to make a difficult sacrifice for someone else? How did it feel?
3. Jordan faced moments of doubt and fear but pressed forward. Can you think of a time when you had to overcome fear to do what you knew was right?
4. What lessons can be drawn from the Water King's final act of sacrifice? How does it reflect values such as humility and selflessness?

find printable learning resources at www.atlischak.com

ACKNOWLEDGEMENTS

The person who deserves all my thanks is the Lord, Jesus Christ. This story is about You, and I wouldn't have been able to write and publish it without Your guiding hand. Thank you!

To my parents, Myron and Tamara, whom I love deeply. I hope this story adequately reflects my affection.

To my twin brother, Nathan, whom I would go as far as Jordan to show my love.

To Lee Bratton, my unofficial go-to beta reader. Your insights, wisdom, support and friendship have helped me greatly.

To those in my local church, Grace Reformed Baptist Church, who have spurred me on to complete this story by words of encouragement and overall example of character.

ABOUT THE AUTHOR

A.T. LISCHAK was born and orphaned in L'viv, Ukraine in 1998. He and his twin brother were adopted one year later by American parents. Lischak grew up in the small town of Brookfield, Ohio until he went to college at Moody Bible Institute in Chicago. There, he received a bachelors degree in pastoral studies in 2021. After an eight-month gap season in New Hampshire, he moved to Owensboro, Kentucky, where he currently lives. He is a member of Grace Reformed Baptist Church.

connect with me on my website
follow me on Amazon & Goodreads

A.T. Lischak

www.ingramcontent.com/pod-product-compliance
Lightning Source LLC
Chambersburg PA
CBHW030600310726
48979CB00003B/516

* 9 7 8 1 9 6 3 2 7 5 0 8 7 *